When in Spain...

JUST ONE OF ANOTHER NEW, AND PROBABLY FINAL, BATCH OF TALES

by

Dick Wild

**Grosvenor House
Publishing Limited**

This book is published by
Grosvenor House Publishing Ltd
Link House
140 The Broadway, Tolworth, Surrey, KT6 7HT.
www.grosvenorhousepublishing.co.uk

A CIP record for this book
is available from the British Library

ISBN 978-1-83975-586-6

For Jane, Rick
& The Kids
[from 2 generations']

Contents

When In Spain

Tee-shirts folded on shelves, bits and bobs put in various drawers in the bedroom, kitchen and bathroom, Bill stepped through the patio door to be greeted by sunlight and the odd sensation of a warm breeze drifting in from the Mediterranean.

Relieved to have put the rigmarole of tickets, airports, luggage and taxi fares behind them – a few days in the sun beckoned: not least...chance to walk around in little more than a pair of knee-length shorts and a floppy vest-like top.

His head turned at a voice from somewhere out back, a voice blurred behind cupboards and kitchen shutters.

'The fridge seems to be working okay.' Helen – his partner – appearing from the kitchenette dressed in similar garb – purple knee length shorts and a skimpy lemon sleeveless top.

'And there's a microwave,' she said, looking over her shoulder. 'And the washing-machine seems reasonably straightforward to operate.'

Good Bill thought, breathing the air and following the progress of what he took to be a cruise ship en-route to the Middle East, or some other port-of-call too distant to be of any huge significance.

'What about the mosquitoes?' She scoured the room for whatever mosquito repellent-gadget-type thing she'd assumed would have been left on the sideboard or stuck in the corner somewhere.

'Mosquitoes,' she said, turning to search the wall and behind the patio-door. 'We ought to get some protection.'

'We'll add it to the list when we go shopping.'

'I don't want to wake up itching like crazy covered in a mass of lumps.'

'We'll put it on the list,' Bill was following a scooter's path skirting the shimmering tip of the hill, its shirt-flapping rider dressed more for a bout of litter-picking on the beach than assuming control of a motorised vehicle.

He turned to where a bottle of *Agua-Con-Gas* lay in wait on a shelf by the fridge. The shuffle of flip-flops passed her by.

Stepping onto the road for the first time was a moment to savour. Chance to *feel* the sun after a morning spent faffing about at airports and clambering in and out of taxis.

Helen held her head back, allowing it to burn into forehead and cheeks. Whilst behind, Bill closed the door and checked he'd got the key safely tucked away in his pocket. He flung the bag over a shoulder. He could do with a beer. Always the same when you first set foot abroad. How long before he could justify cracking open his first bottle of *Pride*? He looked at his watch. Another three hours at least.

'Half these places seem empty,' Helen remarked, observing a line of shuttered villas half concealed behind fences whilst trying to master the art of avoiding loose stones finding their way inside her flip-flop. Bill looked to where a line of half-built timber supported frames lined an adjacent hillside, his eye settling on a sliver of silver that was the far-flung horizon of the Mediterranean.

The *Supermercado* was a half hour walk along a straight road that a quarter mile or so further would take you into the centre of town. A walk not to be underestimated clad in a pair of flip-flops and a loose-fitting top, and in temperatures threatening to glue you to the spot if you failed to keep moving – with or without the company of a steady convoy of trucks and scooters.

The *Supermercado* was cool and, at this time of year, doing a brisk trade. First thing you noticed – the language, evident in its barrage of signs, offers, adverts. Helen had the list, Bill followed close at hand pushing the trolley. The 'essentials' went in first: bread rolls, milk, lunch stuff: ham, cheese, tomatoes, tea-bags, as many agua-con-gases as could be comfortably negotiated. Then a few *luxuries*, though hardly luxuries in any real sense of the word...wine, brandy, vodka, chocolate for late night *lumumbas* on the balcony. San Miguels...bottles of. Sugar, mosquito repellent, sun-cream...*to be bought at the destination rather than before travelling.*

They strode casually towards the delicatessen counter: an impressive display – lines of glazed hams hanging from the ceiling dripping into cups hooked to their base.

No less impressive was the beer shelf. Newcastle Brown's, Pride's, Abbot, the obligatory line of *San Miguels*. He loaded the trolley, toying with a *Hefeweizen* but deciding against – a bit on the heavy side in this heat.

Stepping from the *Supermercado* into an even warmer breeze, Helen took one bag, Bill took the other two.

'You okay?'

'Yeh.'

'Careful stepping onto the road.' With them driving on the other side, he made a point of checking in both directions. He followed her.

'Phew...!' Helen stopped to pull her shoulder strap back into place and stretch her neck.

Walking behind gave him ample chance to view her calves – bare to a point a few inches above the knee. Bare shoulders too – skimpy top clinging to her by a couple of strands. But no way close to doing anything for him. Not in these temperatures. And at this time of day walking down the road carrying bags of shopping. It was enough to be concentrating on walking in a straight line, avoiding trucks and scooters ridden by kids.

'Feel that hot breeze.'

Bill stared out to sea. Sometimes blue, sometimes silver. Nearly always still. Today – as still as a mirror. He looked at his watch. Change of plan – get rid of the shopping then down to the beach and straight into the sea.

The bags were sorted in the kitchenette.

'Looking a bit more lived-in.'

Bill put the beers in the fridge. Brandy in the top cupboard. The ice-cube rack filled from the Agua-Sin-Gas bottle and placed in the freezer. Never tap water.

'Hungry?'

He wasn't really, but maybe a roll and a bit of cheese. Few more hours it'd be time for a beer.

Helen went to the mirror to examine the right side of her face. She wasn't sure if she'd been bitten walking to the *Supermercado*. Bill drank a glass of agua-con-gas.

'What about the mosquito repellent?' She looked over her shoulder. And then turned back to the mirror.

Bill was back on the balcony, blinking in the sun and shifting the white plastic table.

'How about watering the plants?'

He took in the view and another drink of agua-con-gas.

Helen took another quick check on the other side of her face.

'What's it like out there?'

'Hot,' he said. 'And it'll be even hotter tomorrow according to the forecast.'

She turned to brush an eyelash from her cheek.

Carrying a bag with a spare towel, lotions, water, biscuits and two bags of crisps, they made their way down the slope through a gap in the restaurants that took them onto the beach, where they removed their tops in as modest a fashion as possible, immediately turning their attention to the basket of goodies.

Being a recent-arrival calls for a degree of diplomacy surrounded by bronzed Adonises and scantily-clad women.

Some engaged in a game of handball that appeared to be the source of much amusement.

Bill rubbed some lotion into Helen's shoulders – suitably positioned to view a bunch of females frolicking in the sun or wrestling with beach-balls, their thighs willowy and supple. A number of them were bare-breasted. He noticed the variety in shape and size. Some firm, some rounded and fuller than others. Some jigging vibrantly when there was a ball to be retrieved or thumped over a net erected for the purpose.

'Interesting viewing?'

Bill opted to keep quiet. There seemed little need to deny noticing the breasts of women and girls who happened to have plonked themselves in the vicinity topless. It wasn't as if it was doing anything for him. Not that at this time of day and in this heat. Plus – you could never be sure how sex featured on their agendas if they were Spanish, which most appeared to be.

Helen's posture remained unchanged – stretched flat on the towel eyelids glued shut to feel the benefit of the sun whilst effectively removing it from vision. Bill turned a pebble in his fingers and tossed it three feet in the direction of another pebble.

'I hope we didn't leave the margarine on the counter.' Helen rotated on the towel to face the sea, exposing her other half to the sun.

A mirror-like sea continued to grab Bill's attention. And he'd forgotten his hat. He looked left and right, contemplating the implications of what would be his first major decision of the day. Eventually launching himself from the towel and heading straight for the water.

'Careful,' Helen had raised herself on her elbows to follow his path to the water's edge. If there'd been a reply she'd failed to catch it. She was back in position before he'd hit the water.

It was on these occasions that he fancied himself as a bit of a swimmer. Well out of his depth but treading the water with ease, warming to the sense of isolation; away from shouting kids and grans displaying all manner of skin ailments. The coastline's bars and restaurants visible but only as a line of match-box figures against a backdrop of mountains shimmering in the heat and in contrast to the valley beneath it, wholly devoid of life.

Breathing deeply encouraged him to think about what he might fancy eating later. Pasta-Place or pepper-steak at Antonio's – two distinct possibilities. Before that – an hour or two on the balcony followed by a few at one of the cafés on or around The Balcon.

He took the plunge to venture a few feet beneath the surface.

'Good?' She'd barely shifted an inch in his absence.

'Yeh – not bad.'

He dried himself and immediately plonked himself on a towel laid flat on the pebbles, the sun forcing him to squint but still enabling him to watch a girl nearby wearing a light dress removed bit by bit, revealing a skimpy thong that failed to come anywhere close to concealing the rounded moons of her buttocks. It was odd how even the flimsiest covering made it seem like you weren't actually viewing women's backsides, when that was exactly what you *were* doing.

Not that it made any real impression. Not at this time of day. She was a mahogany brown, as was the guy she was with. He said something and she laughed. She had rolled the dress off her and seated herself on the pebbles to roll it into a ball which was put in the basket at her side. She then squirted a generous measure of lotion into the palm of her hands and started spreading it liberally over both breasts.

'Interesting viewing?'

He guessed he'd got away with it. If women were given to stepping out of dresses and rubbing lotion into their breasts it was hardly his problem.

Being their first day, five-o-clock saw them seated under a café umbrella. Helen fancied she'd browned a fraction, if only across the ridge of her shoulders.

The waiter approached. Bill used his Spanish; sufficient to order two beers and two agua-con-gases. He'd been to Spain before – on more than one occasion. He fancied the waiter was a bit put out they hadn't ordered a three-course meal.

'Quite a few Germans.' Helen had noticed one of many signs advertising the restaurant's offers in English and German.

Bill turned to his first beer.

'Phew!' Helen eased herself back into the rear of the chair, eyes closed.

It *was* hot and with little sign of it relenting. The sweat was beginning to roll off him.

The beer was cold and yellow and full of frothy bubbles. But he'd get used to it. He didn't really have much choice. He wasn't really a wine man apart from maybe a glass of red with his meal. Helen had turned her face to the sky.

'What do you fancy eating?'

'Don't mind.'

'Pasta-Place?'

'If you fancy.'

She'd found a gap in the awning, allowing a shaft of sunlight to spill onto her quarter of the patio.

Two girls in bikinis strutted past hand in hand. A bronzed chap with jet black hair and dressed in a suit called something in Spanish they either didn't hear or didn't want to hear.

Bill took another drink of beer. *San Miguel.* If anything he preferred the *Cruzcampo* or *Victoria* which he'd always thought was an odd name for a Spanish beer and one he'd only ever seen at Malaga bus station.

Next round Helen did the ordering, the words tripping off her tongue like a native.

A woman, mid-twenties or maybe younger, possibly Spanish or maybe Italian – occupied a seat at the far side of the patio. She was wearing a pair of shorts the hemline of which reached to just below her buttocks or the top of her thighs depending which way you looked at it. She had a leg raised on another seat, her head held back against the sun.

As the drinks arrived, a guy you assumed hailed from somewhere in North Africa made his way up the steps armed with an array of watches, cigarette lighters: a tray full of stuff he guessed no-one would show the slightest interest in. But he managed a smile – likely some consolation for being as ignored here as at every other venue on his list.

'Hungry?'

He wasn't really. He checked with his watch.

A family had seated themselves round the adjacent table. Spanish; the eldest male – presumably the father – sporting a thick black moustache. His wife was dressed a lightweight floral dress and purple headband. Their youngest kid clutched a chair leg, staring continuously at Bill and Helen, intrigued by the pale-looking couple who – compared to his parents – didn't seem to talk much.

Back at the villa, the heat had prepared its own welcoming party. Bill stepped onto the balcony if only to breathe a little air. At this time of day the strip of sea was visible, but seemed more distant above a line of orange clay rooftops, the houses beneath now caught in temporary shade.

All indications were she was about to shower. The clock was showing six-thirty. One of the advantages of being on holiday – time barely seeming to matter.

He took a sip of *Pride*, allowing a few minutes to lapse before placing the glass on the table to turn to the patio door, closing the shutters behind him.

He heard the swish of the shower spray, positioning himself by the sideboard to wait for the noise to cease which meant she'd be finished. It was a minute or two later that the door opened.

He watched her emerge from the bathroom, hair wet and matted. A towel clinging to her, dripping tiny pools onto the tiled floor. She stepped into the centre of the room, turning to face the mirror.

Moving to within touching distance he raised a hand to make contact with her shoulder. She moved to pull the towel more tightly. His eyes followed her examining her reflection in the glass, checking first the left then the right side, under each eye-brow.

He made his move, placing himself directly behind her, his hand resting – then tightening on her towelled midriff, a prelude to landing a kiss on the nape of her neck.

She shifted from him, his arms back to their former position. She turned from the mirror.

His eye followed her to a nearby table.

'Too hot,' she said, sorting through the contents of a box and speaking in a voice she knew ran the risk of sounding feeble.

He stood his ground a while, watching her examining labels before reaching for a tube of something and removing the lid.

He let the moment pass, turning to take something from one of the drawers and immediately heading for the shower, welcoming the sensation of rushing water, eyes shut tight. Afterwards reaching for a towel and stepping into the room feeling almost cool, heading for the balcony where Helen was already in position, dressed in a flowery top and baggy leggings, her eye on the distant strip of sea.

He retreated to the kitchen where seconds later a top could be heard being wrenched from a beer bottle.

Post-shower the mood automatically switches to evening mode. The donning of fresh clothing, glasses filled. Chance to reflect on the day so far and picture the night ahead: taxi booked for seven. Restaurant about eight-thirty, following a few at one of the cafes around The Balcon.

Bill finished his beer and stepped to the kitchen to replenish his glass, swiping the top off the bottle and discarding it in the rubbish beneath the sink. Following the café earlier he'd probably be a bit pissed after this one but so what? That's what holidays were for.

Night time – or early evening – the cafes made for lively viewing: couples sauntering arm in arm, families, kids hankering after the round-town tour by train or ice-creams.

A couple of lads passed by flinging a ball at each other in the expectation the other might drop it and look silly in front of so many people. Helen had drunk a few more than she'd planned at this stage of proceedings but sod it. She leant back in her chair, face levelled at what passed for a breeze wafting in from The Balcon's restaurants and cafes.

'Not so bad now – the heat,' she said, her eyes closed.

Bill nodded and took a drink of beer.

On leaving the café they walked slowly. It was some fifty yards after leaving their seats that she took his hand and a few yards later that his fingers closed round hers.

At the Pasta-Place they had to wait a few minutes to be seated which wasn't unusual at this time of night. Though whether the food was any better was a matter of conjecture.

'Busy.' Helen had her eye on a table in the corner that she hoped might be free when their turn came round. 'What do you fancy to eat?'

He hadn't given it much thought. Chicken...*Pollo* or whatever it was called; if his memory served him right – served in a kind of herby sauce.

'What about you?'

'Not sure.' She curled a lip to give it some thought. 'Possibly lasagne.'

Helen went for wine with their meal whilst Bill stuck to beer. They brought bottles automatically which was unusual. Maybe with it being a restaurant rather than a bar. General consensus was the bottled *San Miguel* had the edge on the draft version but in his book there was still something to be said for drinking beer from a tap.

Helen's side-on posture enabled him to view her choice of evening wear: not so straightforward a decision as one might imagine: a loose floral top with baggy sleeves – in these temperatures hardly surprising. It was tied at the top which meant the curve at the top of her breasts was visible – deliberately or accidentally was difficult to say. It depended on the size of the breasts. Helen's were about average. They tended to droop slightly but not to the point of sagging. She'd opted for a pair of baggy slacks to match the top, making her lower half fairly anonymous and making little impression on him one way or the other. Earrings were her speciality, especially on holiday. Tonight's was a cluster of butterflies dangling from a hook.

'Phew....' She wafted herself with the menu. Eating had a habit of making you hotter.

A bit of people-watching comes with the territory. And at this time of night, the bars and cafes around The Balcon and the surrounding lanes and thoroughfares provided every opportunity: Spanish, Dutch, German, English. Certainly English. The location always a popular venue for the Brits seeking their two weeks in the sun. It was odd how proximity to one's compatriots prompted a degree of apprehension. The all-too-familiar voices a bit too close for comfort and making you wonder what they'd come out with next, or at what volume. If they were Spanish or Dutch you'd hardly notice, or care.

'We need to get the mosquito repellent sorted out when we get back.' Helen eased herself into her seat, arms straightened to examine a shade or two of brown in the elbow region. Bill was following a waitress dressed in black delivering a plate of what he assumed was paella to a table in the neighbouring restaurant.

Helen's plan to go easy on the gin & tonics was being put to the test. The problem was the measures; all they did was tilt the bottle. So if she was already half pissed it wasn't entirely her fault. What she didn't want was to be suffering the following day – their first full day.

It was always a relief to get the 'eating bit' done and dusted, enabling you to crack on with the main business of the evening: a tour of three or four bars up a cobbled street that at this time of night was packed to a point of heaving. A relief to make it to your first port-of-call and no less a relief to be ordering yet another *Cerveza...!*

They sat outside observing waiters scurrying back and forth and passers-by staring leisurely into shop windows. Women – girls – seeming to be everywhere; their bronzed limbs darkened considerably under the lights of the street's bars and restaurants. Not that Bill was deliberately looking. He just happened to be looking in that direction. He had as much of an eye on the Cocktail-List that would likely feature at some point over the next few days.

A private prediction that Helen would struggle to make it beyond their third port-of-call proved not far wide of the mark. Twenty minutes after taking their seats her eyes began doing their 'lizard impression' – opening and closing in rapid succession and not entirely of their own volition.

It meant their fourth stop-off point would almost certainly be their – or *her* – last. They'd named it *The Pink Bar* on account of its garish seat covers. On their last visit they'd got on speaking terms with a woman who was there again this year: an Australian girl working behind the bar; one of those well-travelled types that made your own life and ambitions seem incredibly unadventurous. Not that Helen was in a state to be engaging in conversation on anyone's ambitions by the time they got round to paying the bill.

It was whilst waiting for the slip of paper to be delivered to the table that her hand reached across the table and after a little fumbling, made contact with his.

'Sorry,' she managed to say, her eyes doing their opening and closing routine in more rapid succession followed by taking a tighter grip on his hand. 'Earlier...you know.'

As usual – it arrived more or less on-cue: the alcohol-induced 'apology' designed to dispel notions of guilt. And warranted or not – too befuddled to carry any strain of conviction.

'It's...the heat...' She was struggling for an explanation she – more than he – knew would hardly hold up to scrutiny. Hence the need to get pissed. With him feeling vindicated in refusing to make it a topic of conversation, switching the subject to the relative safety of the following day's agenda. There'd be little call for any discussion there.

Carol, the Aussie, arrived with their change. She looked at Helen and cast a knowing smile at Bill who returned the smile – Helen, by that point, pretty much oblivious to it all.

The walk to the taxi rank was a struggle but they eventually made it. They'd forego a few on the balcony; maybe the following night.

Having negotiated the cab and appropriate fare with a tip and managed to get the right key in the right lock, they made their way to the kitchen where Bill insisted she down four glasses of agua-sin-gas before heading for the bedroom, lending a hand to getting her sorted and in a position to collapse into bed. She tried grasping his hand.

'Sorry...you know...earlier.' He nodded – her tendency to repeat herself when pissed another habit best ignored.

Bill led her to bed, coaxing her into place.

As was often the case on holiday, he wasn't ready to call it a day just yet. It wasn't unusual for him to pop off to a late night bar on his own last thing at night. She understood and had no problem with that. It was, after all, *both* their holidays!

'You go...' She went so far as to wave him on his way. 'You enjoy yourself...And don't drink too much.' She was giggling even as she said it.

It was halfway through the door that he remembered the mosquito-repellent. They'd deal with it in the morning.

Outside it wasn't so much hot as pleasantly warm. He liked this time of day, or night – feeling a bit pissed but not absolutely pissed. Still time for a few more; the question was where?

Taxis were available twenty-four/seven from the hotel on the road to town; the casino-hopping clientele making it worth everyone's while to have someone permanently available, the first vehicle in the queue dropping him back in the centre only forty minutes after they'd left it.

He stood on a corner close to the taxi-rank, looking for signs of a suitable watering-hole.

Whilst knowing he'd wind up in the German Bar. Towards the centre but up a few streets. The place they'd found last time, proving to be the ideal final-port-of-call where you could actually get a decent German beer, Warsteiner if his memory served him right.

He concentrated on keeping to the side, walking in a straight line, knowing one of the pitfalls of being a bit pissed was that you were often more pissed than you imagined.

The bar had a weird name, more Spanish sounding than German, the dark-wood interior almost a throwback to pubs back home, indication this was where the real drinking was done once the cafes and restaurants had closed. Football memorabilia and flags adorned the walls, Bayern Munich featuring on more than a handful of occasions. There were a few empty stools at the side in addition to a few tables. He could do without having to stand. They'd also serve you at the bar, often more convenient than trying to get the attention of late-night waiters in cafes.

It was the same guy behind the bar as on their last visit, the owner's son so the story went. On the beer front things couldn't be simpler – Warsteiner...Large! He used his bit of German, partly because he was pissed and partly to come across as a cosmopolitan well-travelled kind of guy, unlike the bulk of their clientele – or so one imagined. As usual it took a while, repeatedly spooning the froth off the top of the glass, the way it should be done.

He found a stool as opposed to a table and hooked his feet onto the rest. It was a mixed clientele: some Spanish guys playing cards, English voices in one corner and a line of German males seated at the bar, smoking – very much a home from home at such an hour and in such surroundings.

The beer arrived, pale and clear, topped with a head of foam. He held it at eye-level, sipping it with the reverence of a man taking his first drink after a long hike across the desert before allowing it to stand on its Brauhaus beer mat.

He took in the surroundings, lifting a German newspaper from a nearby rack to see what, if any, sense he could make of its headlines.

'May I?' The voice belonged to a youngish-looking female hovering by his shoulder, German from the sound of it. She was indicating the tool next to him, seeking confirmation it was okay to sit there. He extended an arm and nodded.

'Thankyou.' She sounded each syllable in the strict Germanic manner you half expected.

He couldn't help noticing her legs: slim and bare and crossed repeatedly on settling into her seat, shoulder length hair tossed from side to side. Smiles led to confirmation the stools on which they were sitting would no way interfere with each other's movements.

Sitting in such close proximity makes conversation inevitable, and – after a few beers – not too much of a strain. Establishing that she was from Cologne, on a kind of holiday though visiting her elderly uncle who lived in one of the villas just out of the centre a kilometre or so away. As was often the case with younger Germans, particularly from the north of the country, her English was impeccable. He took his turn to fill her in on his circumstances – hesitating before mentioning Helen, but then going on to explain that she'd gone back to the villa – pissed. He mimed the action which got the predictable amused reaction.

The girl – or woman given her age, though she somehow had the look of a younger female – was called Ava. As well as practising her English she insisted it was good to have someone English to talk to; someone to put her right if she said something incorrect. A look in his direction an indication he wasn't to opt out of his obligations in this respect.

Another toss of hair drew attention to her face: sultry in a vaguely adolescent vein: a face devoid of make-up and totally at home dressed in a simple loose-fitting top that was little more than a vest and a pair of equally revealing cut-down jeans, the bared legs difficult to ignore even if you tried.

What Bill was fairly sure of though he wasn't quite in a position to confirm it, was that she wasn't wearing a bra – the contours of a small pair of breasts against the fabric of her top clear enough from where he was sitting.

He talked about the place they were staying in for a few days, a place they'd rented a few kilometres away as her belated birthday treat. And a bit about where he came from in England, or more where they were currently living and working – one of the outer London boroughs. Her home town being Cologne was convenient; his having visited the place a few times: once on a stop-over on the way to Munich and on another occasion to take in the local beer scene...Kolsch and then a few kilometres up the line to Dusseldorf...Alt beer territory!

Between drinks he made a point of complimenting her on her English which she was quick to assure him was no big deal for a German having studied English at school and university and being brought up on a diet of English on radio and in films and music. Plus – it was good for her to practise her English with an English person, as long as the person didn't mind. Another quick check in his direction as she turned to finish her drink.

Time for another beer, always better ordered in the speaker's native tongue, listening and watching her turn on her stool to attract the attention of the barman – an action causing breasts to jiggle and legs bared to just beneath the buttocks to be crossed and re-crossed.

The beers arrived, followed by the chink of raised glasses – evidence that she too was some way down the line to getting pissed. And something of a novelty to be with a woman for whom beer, as in ale, was the drink of choice. And who proved to be quite an expert on the subject, her accounts of brewing techniques – very much the German tradition – quickly losing Bill.

With the bar rapidly filling she'd shifted slightly, her legs still crossed but squeezed into even more limited space with the adjacent stools now occupied, her breasts still showing a tendency to wobble with each lifting of her glass – the wad of hair tossed repeatedly from her face apparently more for effect than serving any real purpose – but a habit you were inclined to overlook.

They talked about Spain and the ex-pat communities – the German contingent having colonised the resort Bill had frequented on a number of occasions a few kilometres down the road. Their brashness, as with many ex-pat communities – largely seen as a syndrome of foreigners attempting to cope in an essentially alien environment.

The Warsteiner was going down well – possibly too well; a tendency he felt no obligation to be drawing a halt to just yet, nor wanted to be paying a too heavy price for in the morning.

She elaborated on her circumstances: aside from visiting her uncle who owned one of the flats close by, how she was chilling-out for a few weeks (her words). And – staring at a glass repeatedly rotated on its mat – a recently curtailed relationship with a man from Dortmund. Which was where she stopped, with little willingness – or inclination – to continue. Just a further toss of hair and raising of a near empty glass to her lips.

Though never a fan of seeking people out on holiday, particularly people like Ava who gave an impression of being a little intense and eager to press you on things you didn't necessarily have any strong feelings about – there were times when you made an exception. Like when it was late at night and you were both drunk. And when she was both a beer drinker and an excellent English speaker. And wore cut-off jeans and went around bra-less beneath a thin cotton top.

Maybe because he was drunk it neither surprised nor irritated him that she pressed him on his relationship with Helen. He had the impression it was the way with many women; that whether or not it was ostensibly any of their business – you made allowances because you sensed a genuine interest with an inclination to see your side of things in the course of discussion.

It was on the arrival of their fourth or fifth beer that warning bells suggested it may be wise to make this their last.

A proposal concurred with on the adjacent seat. Which raised the subject of her getting back to her uncle's place – a half mile detour from the centre, a route that took her along the sea-front for what, by day, was one of her favourite walks.

She'd stood from her stool, stretching her legs and checking her ability to go to the bar and pay.

Bill lifted his bag from the stool and made his way to the door.

Outside, the street seemed darker than before, and much cooler after the smoky atmosphere of the bar.

Aware of the sound of their own footsteps on a now deserted street they took an alleyway that led them past a line of upturned tables chained in stacks of five outside a shuttered cafe. A street that, in turn, led them to a path which took them to the seafront, where a left turn formed another path taking them up an incline to a grassy track only feet from the cliff.

Twice they stopped for her to assure him she'd be okay. That in a place where crime was rare and tourists rarely targeted, a coast-path at night was one of the safest places to be. But Bill either wasn't sure, or was too considerate – or just too drunk. Leaving a woman in cut-off jeans and a skimpy top to her own devices at this, or *any* time of night wasn't really on wherever you were. It would be no trouble to see her a bit closer to home.

They walked the coast-path, keeping each other from the edge with exaggerated tugs of arms, avoiding a tendency to step off-course but taking the opportunity to step a little closer in the process. She was more pissed than she'd given the impression in the bar; all the more reason to make sure she got back okay.

He too was stumbling a bit, which made it a good idea to park themselves on a bench; chance to sit a while watching the moon reflecting on the mirror-like surface of the sea.

Not for the first time that day Bill found his eyes drawn to the lights of a passing ship.

Her eyes were on the ship too – and the water.

Until they shifted, along with the rest of her – a shift sufficiently negotiated to rest her head lightly on Bill's shoulder – his head shifting in response, coming to rest lightly amongst locks of hair, their upturned faces only inches apart.

Drawing him towards her, she kissed him in a way both knew had little to do with parting gestures after a few drinks in a bar.

His hand reached to meet her. And meeting little resistance ventured slowly across the cotton top, beneath which the small breasts, almost settling into the palms of his hands, were confirmed as bra-less. Her hand followed suit, taking its own leisurely stroll to the waistband of his shorts – and then beneath.

Motioning him to rise from the seat, she led him to a path that descended sharply, taking them twenty or thirty yards to a plateau surrounded by brambles, vines and a thicket of trees that excluded all but a fraction of light.

On reaching a corner where the ground dropped to a stream they stopped.

Whatever reservations Bill may be having – cut short by arms cradling his neck and on release, beginning a mutual unbuttoning process that soon had what few garments were worn in a small heap on the ground – Ava's slim moonlit body springing instantly to view.

He was urged to join her, sinking to his knees, a hand reaching over the curve of his shoulder.

'Look I___'

'Sssshh___'

A second hand pressing on the other shoulder silenced him, Seconds later he was on his back, stalks of grass, twigs: dried, bunched-up grass – pushing into the flesh of his back and spine.

'Ssshh___'

This time it came as an instruction; hands and fingers rapidly taking control, as did the rest of her, the stiffened tips of her breasts brushing back and forth against the milky pale skin of his chest.

Until a few minutes later, she knelt above him in what was clearly a preferred position, manoeuvring to take him inside her – her breasts trembling through his fingers as she leant, allowing his tongue to take over where his fingers had left off....

Their movements came easily, as did her sighs – muscles contracting in perfect time, coupled with reassurances that everything was fine – that there were no risks; that she knew what she was doing. Leaning to meet him until straightening, searching his eye to witness the pained expression, a signal to bring what remained of their evening to a shuddering halt.

Their dressing was quick, undertaken in near silence – down to circumstance as much as any reflection on what had just taken place.

Back on the path she reassured him what remained of her walk was neither here nor there, confirmed by a quick toss of hair and brief kiss on the lips.

After which – and without reference to possible future meetings – she was halfway down the path in the direction of her uncle's villa.

He stumbled along his bit of path, mumbling to himself about keeping in line, to focus only on getting back to the centre, back to the few remaining lights of the street, trying not to burden himself with the implications of one of the corniest clichés in the book. The one where you were on holiday, met a woman in a bar and ended up fucking with her. Even though that wasn't telling the whole story. That it hadn't gone quite like that. That – on reflection – he knew he'd been pissed before he'd arrived at the bar, as had she, though *how* pissed was impossible to say.

Which wasn't an excuse so much as a reason. And far from an attempt to try and gloss over what had happened.

He found himself repeatedly going over the same ground, striving to find some way through his inebriated state whilst trying to remember the street to get him to where the taxis waited.

Whilst convincing himself he wasn't quite so drunk now. Which was or wasn't true but was some way of focusing his mind. Ava had definitely been drunk. That much he knew for certain. She'd been easily as drunk as him which – as he stumbled on – maybe partly explained what had happened.

Almost by accident he found himself on the road where the 'all-night' taxi rank was fortunately fitting its description.

Maybe she'd taken what he'd been saying about Helen as a cue, though he couldn't remember exactly what he *had* said, apart from touching on details that were as much to do with how much he'd drunk as what he'd probably intended to say. Maybe the whole thing had been down to him; that she'd simply put two and two together and come up with what she construed to be her good deed for the day. And – encountering little resistance.

All of which could be true or mere conjecture. The only certainty – wandering along a street pissed or half-pissed at close to one-thirty in the morning was hardly the time or place to be agonising over such things.

He attempted to focus on arriving back at their villa, negotiating the cab-fare in advance to get the right denomination including a tip. Thankful that, on arrival, the driver proved to be a patient man.

Minutes later he stood – relishing being reduced to wrestling with the collection of keys; confirmation he'd at least made it home but making sure he had the right one at hand, avoiding rattling it in the door as he turned it slowly. And entered without tripping over the step or kicking anything.

The door opened. Along with the realisation he was back in their own four walls; and with his partner.

He headed for the kitchen. Four agua-sin-gases – then the bathroom, no flushing the bog. Still stumbling and stepping out of his shorts, he reached his side of the bed where he slipped beneath the duvet, close enough but not too close to Helen whose snores were audible and whose day had come to a far less complicated conclusion something close to three and a half hours ago.

When he woke he was glad Helen wasn't next to him. But it was a temporary reprieve.

'So – how are you?' The stressing of 'you' had him immediately on the defensive. Had she been awake when he'd got back after all?

He rubbed sleep from his eye and looked to where sunlight was spilling in through the bedroom window. She'd brought him a cup of tea.

'Where did you get to?'

He concentrated on taking the cup from her without dropping it, aware of the need – even at this stage – to think carefully about his answer.

'Found the German Bar.' There was little need to deny everything. They'd discovered the bar together on their last trip and would certainly wind up there at least one of the remaining nights – a prospect best put to one side for now.

'Oh...right.' She sounded vaguely interested. 'Still the same guy working there, the owner's son?'

'Think so yeh.'

'We can go there tonight if you like.' A logical enough suggestion – or an attempt to put him on the spot before he'd even got out of bed.

'Could do.' Which was all he could think to say. She'd gone to the kitchen.

'We forgot the mosquito repellent.'

He stood, pulling on his shorts, resolved to making the day to come as uneventful as possible.

In light of which, a day on the beach wasn't a bad prospect. *Good* to be in a crowd. *Bad* if Ava happened to be amongst the crowd. Though he was pretty certain that was unlikely. He'd got the impression lounging on a beach getting a tan were hardly her thing.

The beach threw up few surprises: the sun a little fresher, the pebbles still too hot to the touch, a game of handball attracting the attention of as many twenty-something males as could gather in such a small stretch of land; the female participants fifty-per-cent bikini-clad – sufficiently tanned and supple in their movements to convince everyone in the vicinity they were getting old – including Bill.

He watched Helen wrestling with a towel, flattening its corners and lying back on the lilo – a purchase they'd treated themselves to at one of the beach shops. He knew that would be her day sorted. Her hangover – severe enough on wakening – now just a listless feeling that was only to be expected on holiday.

He turned his attention to the sea, today as still and clear as glass.

The only issue was how far out of his depth he was going to get. On this occasion – as far as possible. He needed space and time to himself. Time to consider the implications of needing to be on his guard every step he took. But for now at least, having only miles of empty water and empty sky for company. An invitation to lie back, turning left and right to take in the full length of the coastline, eyeing a tiny spot a few hundred yards from the nearest building. Screwing his head further so he could just about make out a stretch of cliff face close to a path. Where, if you ventured late at night, you'd come across a small plateau surrounded by bushes and trees.

It was with a sharp intake of breath and a swift backward somersault that he disappeared beneath the surface.

'Okay?'

'Yeh...not bad.' He dabbed himself with a towel, amazed how people seemed able and/or motivated to lie for hours in the sun without getting bored or burning half to death.

The game of handball was in full flow. He watched as he re-took his seat – turning to retrieve a bag of crisps buried somewhere amongst lotions and bottles of agua-sin-gas.

Preparing for their second night out was no less a performance than for the previous night. Choosing the right top to match the right bottom that, on this occasion was a pale lemon, which meant a top with nothing yellow in it. And meant the beads and earrings came from a different batch. What didn't vary greatly was the make-up except for a slightly darker blue on each eyelid.

'What do you think?'

Bill had retired to the balcony with his first bottle of *Newcastle Brown*. She was stood in the gap of the door, make-up applied, earrings chosen to go with the sleeveless top.

'Okay.' Which, as a response, would suffice – gestures of approval neither required nor expected. She was already halfway back to the kitchen to sort out her first g&t of the evening.

Watching her make her way to the kitchen brought home what they both knew; that the evening get-up was ultimately a sham: the beads, the earrings, the baggy slacks, painstakingly applied make-up – all an attempt to show one side of herself whilst serving to conceal another side: a side that always had and always would be beyond reach – or discussion.

She was beside him, glass in hand.

'What do you fancy eating?'

He'd barely thought about it.

'Don't know…maybe fish.'

She pulled the chair closer.

'You okay?'

He turned to face her.

'You seem a bit pissed-off.' She was adjusting an earring with the fingers of one hand.

'No I'm fine. I was just thinking if not fish I could maybe manage a pepper-steak.'

She fingered the other earring and took a drink.

'How about you?'

'Not sure…maybe tuna.'

From the first bar – or café, as it tended to be at that time of the evening – Bill had the sensation of being the centre of everyone's attention. That he was the one who'd got off with a German girl. And then sneaked his way home in a cab to make it seem like nothing had happened. All behind his partner's back: the one next to him leaning back in her chair with her eyes closed, oblivious to it all.

Helen reached for her glass.

'I was just thinking. For my sister's wedding I might treat myself to a new outfit. I've got the one from Hilary's engagement do last year but it was a bit heavy…as in weight.'

Bill could vaguely picture the outfit in question but had little to say on the subject. Which was fine by her. Like most conversations on such matters he wasn't expected to have an opinion, only to listen while she did her bit of thinking aloud. Ultimately just something to pass a little time. She drank and placed the glass on the table.

'I think they'll be okay when they get their flat sorted out.'

Back to her sister and her fiancé. He'd met them a few times. As a couple they were okay. Neither had anything of any real interest to say but that could apply to a whole host of people you were obliged to pass the time of day with on occasions. They were currently looking for a place to buy which, when decorated from top to bottom with this bit knocked out there and this bit added here – re-fitted kitchen – would be marked out as *their place.* Until the time came to move to a bigger place which – when decorated from top to bottom with this bit knocked out there and this bit added here – another re-fitted kitchen – would also be *their place.* And would be the time to start thinking about a family. He'd occasionally tried picturing the pair having sex. It was what sometimes crossed his mind when meeting couples for the first time; the ones you couldn't imagine screwing. Like her other sister who lived in Gravesend. He couldn't imagine her screwing. And *certainly* couldn't imagine screwing her.

He reached for his glass. Helen was trying to catch the eye of the waiter to order the next round.

Couples were everywhere. He'd been observing their movements and mannerisms; the linking fingers as opposed to holding hands – a show of togetherness but without going over-the-top about it. As a rule Bill wouldn't bother with either – but on vacating their seats it was only a short walk to the next bar and they'd be parking themselves there for at least one drink if not two or three.

On arrival and without need for discussion the drinks were ordered, a pattern for the evening already taking shape. He knew to watch his step. She'd already remarked that he seemed a little quiet and with a few drinks inside her might be inclined to press him were he to persist. He'd assured her it was just the heat. And made a pact with himself to avoid extended silences.

'They need to get more fans.' Helen pulled her sleeve, shaking the folds in the puffed out bits near the wrists. She let one sleeve drop and examined the other.

'We could eat paella tomorrow.'

'If you fancy.'

'Odd how they only seem to do it for two.'

'Probably something to do with the ingredients.'

'And the fact they sometimes need twenty-four hours' notice.'

She had a point. Sometimes you had to give twenty-four hours' notice if you wanted to eat paella. Which meant they'd have to find somewhere where you didn't have to give twenty-four hours' notice. Or they could get to the restaurant first thing in the morning and book it there and then, in which case they'd be giving them twelve hours' notice. Maybe that would suffice. Bill had never been overly fussed about Paella – too much pissing around trying to get bits out of shells.

Though *The Pink Bar* would prove safe enough territory Bill was struggling to settle. Not least with events from here-on being largely out of his hands aside from following Helen's example of the previous evening, suggesting they retire early for a few on the balcony back at the villa – which he'd known from the moment he'd woken was no way going to happen.

Which made developments half an hour or so after taking their seats something of a turn-up for the book.

He'd been aware of her lapsing into one of her silences – which meant a number of possibilities.

In this case it led to her reaching for his arm.

He made a point of leaning to listen.

'Would you mind if I went back?'

The question – or more her intention – came out of the blue and caught him entirely off guard. But he instantly knew the need to play it down – answering only to check he'd heard her correctly.

Her grip tightened, taking his expression to be one of frustration that their second evening seemed destined to end in similar fashion to the first.

'Do you mind?'

'Well – if you're sure.'

'I'm thinking taking it easy on the first two nights wouldn't be a bad idea after all the sun and maybe tomorrow we could

go to Friguana, have a few at lunch time at one of the bars.
Maybe have lunch there.'

He took his time answering, happy to concur with whatever
suggestion sprang to mind.

'You sure about this. I don____'

The hand tightened.

'You stay. There's no point in the pair of us schlepping back
and then you getting a taxi back. I'm okay, nowhere near as
pissed as last night. And if I get back and feel like one more I
can always go on the balcony. '

'Well – if you're sure you'll be okay getting back.'

It got a wave of an arm.

'Don't worry. I'll be fine.'

The finances were easily sorted. She left the agreed amount
on the table and leant to reach for her bag.

'It's your holiday too remember.'

It was as she crossed the table to say her goodbye that her
arm circled his neck.

'I love you...' She reached to land a kiss in the middle of his
cheek.

'Okay...' he said, wondering if he should return the
compliment and kiss her back. Either was an easier option than
he'd been facing fifteen minutes ago. He kissed her on the cheek.

'Just – be careful,' he said.

'Just remind me which street up is the taxi-rank?' She
looked up but without relinquishing her grip on his arm. He
gave her the directions, watching her steady herself and make
her departure through a maze of tables and chairs, disappearing
seconds later into the crowded street.

Bill caught a wry smile as Carol reappeared. He could have
explained that it wasn't quite the same as the previous night
but instead he offered the plate, waiting for her to thank him
for the tip.

A brisk walk seemed a good idea: chance to stretch his legs
and give his next move some serious thought, before he got
too pissed.

He took a left away from the main drag, making it to the top of the street then retraced his steps and headed for another bar that he and Helen had discovered on their last visit. A place they'd termed *Belgian Benny's*: a Dutch bar run by a chap called Ken and his French wife Maite and an English chef called Adrian – only a five minute walk away but with alcoves at one end where he could hopefully plant himself beyond view of the street.

On arrival he headed straight for the rear with only a passing glance at the bar to confirm his order.

Taking his seat he gave some thought to what might follow, that whatever transpired – which he'd have to concede would be as much in Ava's domain were she to appear on the scene – could no way be defended, either in terms of what was happening between them or the situation between him and Helen. That these-things-happen – sounded as limp now as it had staggering along the cliff-top in the early hours of the morning. But, given the situation, with only a few days remaining before going home – how else was he to view it? Fact was, these things *did* happen, whether it be women or guys. Like viewing women on the beach or in bars at night. With your partner close at hand who'd come out with comments like 'interesting viewing'? Which was her way of acknowledging you were bound to notice these things and might be getting turned-on by some of what you were seeing. Which happened; no matter where you were: any resort in any country. But would be overlooked because you were on holiday – just like everyone around you was on holiday. And, as they say – these things happen.

Which for now would do as an explanation. That another was waiting in the wings any time he chose to take advantage of it – would be put to one side for now.

Forty-five minutes later he downed what remained of his drink and asked for the bill.

He entered the bar determined to remain anonymous. The subdued lighting helped. He noticed a different man behind the bar: different but unmistakably German – the layered hair a dead give-away.

He ordered his beer. It would be brought over. He looked for a place to sit. The stools were taken but a small table in the corner was empty. The area round the bar was busy, busier than before but as with most late-night bars hardly frequented by those seeking to strike up conversations with strangers.

He crossed the floor, reaching to take a newspaper from the rack: a German red-top, similar in tone of any of its sister publications – dishing up its diet of crap but at this time of day an easier read than the 'quality' end of the market.

He turned the page, paying scant attention to anything it said, rehearsing and re-rehearsing what he might say or what line he might adopt were Ava to appear on the scene. Casual, but friendly. Not surprised to see her again. But not necessarily expecting it.

It was something like fifteen minutes after taking his seat that he got a chance to put it into practice.

He looked up, meeting a familiar voice with a semi-surprised expression.

'Hi.' Remember me?'

'Oh...hi.' Surprised, shocked. Either proved immaterial as – on arranging the chair opposite – Ava leant the full width of the table to kiss him fully on the lips.

He put the newspaper to one side, watching as she settled into her seat, legs as slim and petite – and bare as the previous night, a mane of hair tossed from her eyes before looking to catch the barman's eye.

Beer ordered – routine conversation took up where it had left off the previous evening, both talking in low voices, the implication – if either chose to see it that way – that their day was likely to pick up from here on.

It was around an hour and a half later that they left the bar, this time with few qualms about walking hand-in-hand – a slightly off-putting feeling despite their being no-one around to witness it.

Almost in silence as if the rituals of early courtship were already behind them, they reached the edge of the path, following its steady incline to where – like the previous night – they took a moment to view the scene: the sea with its distinct metallic-look – a fitting backdrop for their opening kiss; and for Bill to test the water – a hand creeping beneath the cotton top met by a more urgent parting of her lips, the signal to abandon their seats and make their descent to the same spot as the previous night.

Undressing in silence, Bill watched, no less awe-struck than twenty-four hours ago, Ava's unclothed body stirring him to heights of arousal he hadn't experienced for some time, urging him to adopt a more active role. Wanting her to know he was no novice in these matters. Though only to a point. He'd already come to accept this was very much Ava's territory: as far as he could gather almost a second home over the last twelve months or so. And that to all intents, he was her guest, expected – and in his case, prepared – to act accordingly, to accept a more subordinate role, to take his place, as instructed, on the grass as she perched herself above him, enabling him to enter her easily – their fucking again coming under a repeated tossing of hair, reassuring him all was well; that, like the previous night, she knew exactly what she was doing. Whilst allowing him to respond in full – his climax evidence enough that what was happening between them was good. That there should be no recriminations.

Fully dressed they returned to the path where a lengthy embrace was confirmation that a relationship, with whatever implications and conditions...had been established though, significantly perhaps, without reference to future meetings.

The walk to the taxi-rank was less fraught than the previous night, whatever doubts or anxieties still lingered dulled by an evening spent in bars.

He negotiated the cab, the correct fare clutched in his grasp some time before arrival, instructing the driver to draw to a halt some way from the villa to avoid risk of disturbance.

It would be the same procedure as the previous night – kitchen, bathroom, finally heading for the bedroom where Helen's snores were again waiting to greet him.

Stepping from his clothes he noted – with some irony – that she was naked except for a white cheesecloth top.

He quietly drew the sheet back to slip into the space beside her.

If you wanted to do the *alternative tourist* bit, you plonked yourself half way down the bus to be ferried to Friguana, one of the numerous *authentic* Spanish villages dotted in the surrounding hillsides. A bus round about mid-morning being your best bet when you'd likely share occupancy with a handful (or if you got lucky, a whole bus-full) of the local womenfolk.

Clad in black and seated at strategic points to have their voices carry some distance...the impression was this was the *real* Spain: a volley of verbal exchanges where any topic was up for grabs with barely a word of what was said having time to register – or even get heard – before responses arrived usually simultaneously from all four corners of the bus.

Seated amongst them, conspicuously clad in hats, shorts and sun-glasses – Bill, Helen and a handful of others slotted self-consciously into roles of casual-observers.

On disembarking – you walked the length of a main thoroughfare admiring a line of whitewashed cottages and the occasional shop where the *Old Spain* was apparently still alive and kicking.

On exploring one or two of the side roads it was time for a coffee. Taken at an authentic-looking place where a few locals – mainly men in caps and ragged trousers were to be spotted adding their bit of authenticity to proceedings.

They found a modicum of shade: a canopy coming adrift at one end where drinks were delivered from a shed-like affair.

Following coffee it seemed the ideal place to sample the local wine they watched being poured from a vessel resembling a milk bottle and appearing to have the consistency of cough medicine mixed with a little Marmite. They agreed to limit themselves to two before finding somewhere to eat.

It was on the arrival of the next round, waiting for the glasses to be placed on the table that Helen asked about the previous evening. For some reason he was grateful for the heat saving his blushes.

Helen appeared not to have noticed.

'Did you get talking to anyone?' She had made a point of turning to face him.

He thought for a moment.

'Got chatting with one guy, German guy. Bayern Munich fan.' He hoped it didn't sound too improbable.

She leant back, head angled at the sun.

'*Weidersehen*'.

Bill turned to face her.

'*Goodbye*'...in German.' She reached for her glass. 'You say it when you're parting company with someone.'

'Or sometimes they say *Tschuss*.'

Bill was content to keep his German to himself for now.

The conversation switched to lunch, something reasonably substantial as they were eating out.

They went for the spaghetti bolognaise. Never a bad choice at lunchtime; a relatively sound base for a few drinks, but not enough to put you off eating later. When they spoke, the alcohol helped, turning the conversation to Helen's mother who'd lived for a while as a single woman in Brighton and was contemplating downsizing to a bungalow somewhere way from the centre of town.

On arrival back in town, an hour or so on the beach didn't seem a bad idea. At least the beach had its distractions. On this occasion a couple in their twenties, possibly Swedish. Each determined to outdo the other in showing what a good time they were having. The girl almost breathless from a fist-locking game that involved the loser planting a firm kiss on the lips of the victor. Another couple arrived settling a few yards to their left. The girl wearing a flimsy top half way between a sash and a sarong. Her stomach was oak-brown and lean and the subject of considerable attention from her boyfriend whose assistance in applying a little lotion to a bared midriff caused her to throw her head midst throws of laughter.

Enough to get Bill back on his feet for his customary afternoon stroll along mostly deserted streets away from the centre. Streets where the temperatures at times made it painful to be in direct sunlight for more than a few seconds.

The road from the beach took him past a line of restaurants and bars to one of the quietest parts of town, largely residential in terms of what one took to be property-development. A part of town where there always seemed to be building going on but usually with little evidence of anything actually happening. Just yards of concrete slabs, multi-layered and supported by scaffolding formed out of what appeared to be lines of tree-trunks flanked by an army of trucks and cement-mixers.

Bill stopped, removing his hat to wipe his forehead and neck. He was only a short walk from the German Bar. He had an urge to view its shuttered doors but thought better of it. Instead he wandered the streets at the top end of town passing a line of expensive-looking residencies set back off the road, each boasting private lawns with an over-the-top artificial green look about them. A right turn brought him back to the more civilised part of town: a line of restaurants leading to a road close to the seafront. He strode past the place with its tables stacked at night but presently open for business – or so one imagined. A left turn followed, heading in the direction of the nearest beach, a half kilometre or so from their own beach where Helen would barely have moved in the forty-five minutes he'd been away.

A slow stroll up the hill followed a familiar path, taking him to the seat where, for two nights running, he'd sat with Ava. The recollection drawing him to the spot between the seat and the path leading away from the cliff edge. The spot where, hidden in the shadow of branches like a scene in one of these *Confessions Pages* – he'd fucked with her. A spot that midway through the afternoon and, by way of contrast, burning under the weight of the sun – conjured up anything but erotic thoughts – the whole area currently little more than a mass of scorched clay and gorse-bushes.

He shaded his view, content to survey the scene from a distance, resisting the temptation to investigate further. It wouldn't seem right at this time of day without Ava there to share the moment with him.

Instead he stuck to the path, shielding his eye from the sun to peer in the direction of a distant line of houses or villas – or however you described them, each fronted by its own balcony.

One of which was Ava's uncle's place. He pondered which it might be, imagining her stepping onto the balcony in a pair of skimpy cut-off shorts, or even a bikini, looking and waving in his direction. Quick to spot and acknowledge him – her one bright spot in an otherwise uneventful day.

With a wipe of his forehead he reached for his bottle of water, emptying a good third of its contents before turning to head back to more populated parts where he would absent himself a while longer by going for a swim. Awarding himself the privilege of drifting to some far off point of the ocean.

The five-thirty slot came as welcome relief. Maybe after a few beers and a few more on the balcony he could test the water for later, but he knew he needed to tread carefully. The last thing he wanted was to enter into discussions that seemed anything other than idle chat.

Throughout the evening, from the first bar of the night to the Chinese restaurant to taking their seats at the *Pink Bar* close to ten-o-clock – Helen was giving nothing away, indications as to whether she would or wouldn't be lasting the distance – despite it being their penultimate night with her, as yet, not having made it to any late-night venues – kept entirely to herself. All he could do was sit it out and wait – the prospect of her accompanying him to the *German Bar* not exactly thrilling him but coming up with an excuse not to go there equally problematical in light of there being no obvious reason for doing so. Which posed the question how Ava would choose to play it if she happened to be there. She wasn't stupid, and she knew about Helen. Which meant the pair arriving on the scene together had always been a possibility. He was glad he'd put her in the picture in that respect.

It was shortly after taking their seats that Helen drifted into one of her introspective moods. He didn't suspect it was linked to the post-shower episode on their first afternoon. Looking back, that had been a mistake – a spur-of-the-moment thing he should have ignored. He'd made no overtures in that respect since.

It was on reaching to pay her half of the bill that whatever doubts he might have had as to how the remainder of his evening might pan-out were finally laid to rest.

'Fancy the *German Bar*?' The question came as no surprise. Neither did his answer.

'Why not?' he said, reaching quickly for what remained of his beer and downing two thirds of it in one go.

They entered the bar at around Bill's usual time. Keen to avoid anyone's eye he placed their order. The possibility of being recognised by one or two of the regulars hadn't escaped him though it was unlikely to be an issue; a relative stranger with a different woman on his arm hardly the stuff of late-night conversation in places such as this. Thankfully it was still pretty busy.

'There's a table free.' Helen had spotted one of the tables close to where he and Ava had sat only twenty-four hours ago.

Being fairly pissed helped, Helen's decision not quite so traumatic as it might have been and knowing throughout the evening that it couldn't be discounted. But as long as he kept a low profile and Ava played her part by staying off the scene, there'd be every chance of getting through the evening unscathed.

Helen sipped her *Warsteiner*. For her, a rare venture in the drinks stakes but one she was prepared to give a go in a place like this. Revisiting a haunt discovered on their last trip seemed to have pepped her up, aided no doubt by several g&t's beforehand. She scoured the memorabilia, showing some interest in the logos and football team photographs, the jokey bar signs and *Stamm Tisch* which, on checking with Bill meant *regulars' table* - a German tradition unlikely to count for much in a place like this.

Bill's attention was elsewhere. He was certain Ava wasn't in evidence, each arrival observed with a glance that he'd tried not to make too obvious. Knowing the importance of keeping the conversation flowing and to avoid looking round as if deliberately seeking distraction.

Throughout it all – possibly a symptom of his paranoia – he'd had the feeling of Helen watching him. Though not in a way he might have imagined. More acknowledgment that this was very much his territory with its German beer and football links. More his cup of tea than the bars and cafes elsewhere. A reminder too that it was his birthday treat – itself indication of the feelings she still had for him: feelings that had been around since their early days and in many respects weren't going to change. Wanting him to be content; aware that for all the rockiness of their relationship – their differences, the occasional falling-out and an admission that things were far from ideal on the physical side – she'd loved this man for some time. And that she wanted him to be comfortable, feeling that she at least owed him that. Symptomatic of an affection that from time to time, and admittedly usually when a bit pissed – wasn't above telling him she loved him.

On Bill's side of the table there was the possibility things were going to be okay. It had been over an hour without Ava appearing on the scene. Though he still couldn't help wondering how he'd react were she to do so, whether he'd be able to resist showing some reaction.

It was on ordering their next drink; Helen insisting on going to the bar to get the attention of the barman given she wanted to order a *cold* Lumumba, as opposed to the hot version some places served automatically, that Bill – taking advantage of her temporary absence – did another quick check on the area round the bar, focusing on the far corner where his attention was caught by a figure half hidden behind a trio of men. A young woman who – on side-stepping the men – to reach for her drink, was clearly visible in cut-off jeans and with shoulder-length hair that was occasionally tossed from shoulder to shoulder.

He immediately looked away, instinctively shielding the side of his face with a raised hand. Frustration not so much at the possibility of being spotted with Helen as having to accept there'd be no way of acknowledging each other's presence. A reminder too that this was *her* bar as well as a place for them to meet in private; that she was at liberty to frequent it as and when she chose and with whoever she pleased.

Helen had resurfaced at the counter and was at the point of issuing her instructions, or trying to – explaining in English, which shouldn't be a problem given all the staff were virtually fluent in English.

He willed the guys Ava was with to disappear off the scene just for a moment. Just long enough to try and catch her eye, to acknowledge the situation they'd found themselves in. That given a choice she'd have nothing more to do with the men she was with and would be sitting with Bill, happy to chat with him and to leave with him later.

But before there was time for her to even look in his direction, Helen was back at the table.

'Think I managed it,' she was saying, tending to something in her purse.

Bill looked but said nothing. In the time it took her to retake her seat, check the contents of her purse and comment on the effectiveness of the guy behind the bar's English – Ava had disappeared. Whether to another part of the bar or from the bar altogether was impossible to say.

'You okay?' Helen couldn't be sure he'd been listening.

He nodded and reached for his beer, a resolve to keep the conversation flowing already showing signs of weakening.

Helen's suggestion shortly after that they make this their last and head for the cab-rank, maybe have a drink on the balcony back at home, seemed – under the circumstances – like the best suggestion he'd heard all day.

No more than ten minutes after ordering their last drinks they were at the bar settling the bill.

'Auf wiedersehen,' Helen turned to the bar staff.

At the bar heads turned, but only briefly. Bill was already through the door and back on the street.

If Friguana was brief respite from the beach, the city some two hours north east, reached only by car or bus, was a full day job.

Bill was no fan of visiting places such as this. Aside from needing to travel by bus – where the vagaries of the country's transport system were all too frequently in evidence – it was one of those places where you 'viewed things': buildings, walls, squares, museums.

But it was Helen's holiday too. On a short break time is of the essence and she'd expressed a desire to see the place this time round as they'd failed to get round to on their last visit.

So Bill went with it, the pair boarding one of the long-distance buses, perfectly serviceable and comfortable, if no way near as entertaining as the Friguana option. Just a handful of tourists, a few couples and families happy to mind their own business. He had his book and Helen had her crime novel (read at a rate of about one a day on holiday).

A lengthy bus ride allows plenty of time to think as you weave your way in and out of resorts varying little along a relatively flat stretch of coastline. Bill was eager to know more about the previous evening. Whether Ava had spotted Helen and consequently made a decision to depart. Or whether she'd intended to go there anyway and pass a little time in whatever circumstances. Which left plenty of room for speculation as to the coming night – their final night.

First task on disembarking was to refer to the guidebook (provided free of charge at the tourist office back in town) and have some kind of a plan. Helen was in charge. And he was more than happy to have it stay that way.

One of its most famous thoroughfares was the first stop – the guide held at arm's length to check she'd got the right parts in mind, its architecture bearing evidence of both Arab and European influence. Listening from a distance Bill caught a few of the details, able to visualise the squabble that had likely preceded it. And whether – following the trend in modern-day Europe – such days could ever return.

That bit done they took their seats at one of the cafes on a square with views of the gardens and a statue of something related to the Alhambra dynasty going back to the earliest days. Chance to rest their feet and for Helen to do a bit of research for the next hour or so. He watched her flick from page to page, wondering if it was something to do with his upbringing or education (or lack-of) – that led to him having little interest in what might loosely be termed *cultural* matters. Or whether he'd feel similarly if it was Ava sitting opposite, guide-book in hand.

Between sips of café-con-leche he got to hear how the place had been established as an independent kingdom in 1238 and was the home of spectacular Moorish art. He made a show of listening whilst pondering ordering a beer. He definitely fancied one. Maybe it was the bus ride.

It had always been the same when it came to anything to do with history. None of what he heard about or read about either interested, surprised or intrigued him. Either at school or since. To him the fact that time passed and things changed was of little consequence. That monarchs, rulers and other supposedly fascinating individuals arrived on the scene and, often non-too-quickly, disappeared from it was neither here nor there: all too far removed from the ins and outs of modern-day life to interest him or make any real impression.

He looked to get the waiter's attention. Waiters in posh cafes were invariably more difficult to attract than at the tourist venues, or at least that was the way it seemed. Certainly more difficult than in the *German Bar*. Maybe it was the uniform.

Helen was not yet done with the guide-book, flicking its corner to pick up where she'd left off. The Kingdoms of Aragon and Castille united by the marriage of Ferdinand and Isabella.

The waiter arrived. With Helen otherwise disposed Bill placed the order.

'*Uno Cerveza por favour y vino blanco.*'

A nod of a head suggested he hadn't been too far wide of the mark. Either that or it was the kind of place where the waiters were told to bow whenever anyone spoke to them.

'*Al hambra* in Arabic means literally, *the red*. Ibn Ahmar rebuilt the Alcazaba and added it to the walls and towers,' Helen explained.

Bill raised an eyebrow. He was feeling the heat and easing himself into what he hoped would be a space for a little breeze to find its way past the neighbouring chairs.

'Aren't you hot?' he asked.

Helen leant into her chair to give it a bit of thought.

'Mmm…a bit. In 1812 it was taken and occupied by Napoleon's forces.'

Bill was looking for the badge on the beer tap. *San Miguel* or *Cruzcampo?* Or – in these less tourist-orientated parts – maybe some yet-to-be-sampled brew.

'What was?'

'The Palace.'

Bill pulled a face. In those days everyone seemed to be after somebody else's property. Or women. Bit like Franco's time and on reflection – much like today. Minutes later a beer and white wine were duly delivered.

'*Gracias.*'

'*De nada.*' Another bow from the hip.

Helen skimmed the page and turned to the next.

'So much to see and so little time to see it.' She put the booklet to one side, raising both arms for examination. Both were close to what might be termed tanned. Sitting at a table was always a better way of judging it.

'I'm not sure about that mosquito repellent. I think I might have picked up a bite.'

With a wander up a few streets, a second coffee at an *Art Nouveau* type place and taking in a few squares, it was back to join the queue for the return trip. The least appealing part of the day but saved to an extent by the scenery: the backdrop of mountains appearing almost white in the heat, whilst through the window opposite, pockets of blue popped in and out of vision behind buildings and numerous dips in the road, out-of-town vineyards lining the route for much of the latter stages.

The last night of any holiday has its downside. You want to go out on a high and make the most of what little time remains but with thoughts of packing and airports never far away.

Being their last night they'd stick to their usual routine: five-thirty café at the beach-bar. Back for a shower and a few on the balcony. Cab back to town and a few at the bar just off The Balcon, one of those small family owned bars that did free *tapas* and tended to be fairly quiet at that time of day.

Final night meant pepper-steak at *Bar Redondo* where the owner bought the meat from some place up in the hills. And made his own pepper-sauce, the recipe for which was to remain a family secret. When it came to getting a decent steak you needed to know your restaurants. Same as getting a decent *Pina Colada*. It was surprising how it varied from one bar to another, some serving it like a glass of squash.

But for Bill there was more at stake than restaurant menus; making the most of what time remained largely out of his hands. It had been a pleasant few days, a generous gesture on Helen's part – but had confirmed what he'd suspected for a while, reflected in time spent sitting on a beach or even in early evening cafes: the whole performance becoming increasingly irksome. Everything seemed to happen so slowly. With Helen, the way it always seemed to be these days. Particularly over the last forty-eight hours, typified by her habit of drifting into bouts of silence. Which effectively turned his thoughts to the night ahead; the possibility of her not lasting the distance, ungrateful as it likely sounded. There'd been times in the past when she'd head home a little earlier on their final night to avoid suffering too much on the journey home.

At the *Pink Bar* Carol the Aussie found time to chat with them a while, outlining her plans to see out the season in Spain and then make her way to Vietnam followed by Japan. She had friends in Tokyo. After which, dependant on funds, she'd be travelling to China. Bill could only sit and listen. It was definitely a generation thing, but also geographical; younger Aussies rarely seeming to be ones for sticking around too long in their own back yard. It made their journey back to the UK seem neither here nor there.

He'd been trying to avoid looking at his watch, allowing the conversation to drift in whatever direction it chose to go. At one point even – would you believe – onto the subject of Christmas. They were in a bar in Spain in mid-summer and they'd managed to get round to discussing Christmas. Fact was he didn't give a damn about Christmas. Given a choice he'd follow the example of animals – bury themselves in the ground till it was over and done with. But he let it pass.

Helen had been sitting quietly for some time, even struggling to make in-roads into her gin & tonic. He felt obliged to check everything was all right.

'You okay?'

She looked across, seeking to catch his eye before answering. 'No – not really.'

He watched a hand ease back and forth across her stomach, waiting for an explanation.

'I hate to say this, but I think I've crossed swords with the infamous dodgy prawn.'

It was a reference to their last Spanish holiday when Bill had been out of action for a day following a pizza in an Italian restaurant. Just the one *dodgy prawn* able to put you out of action for as long as it takes your system to recover.

She leant across to speak.

'Sorry to say this but I think I need to go back. Maybe I'll be okay if I get some of that *Gavison* stuff or whatever it is, down me. I don't actually feel sick, just a bit queasy.'

She reached across, a hand reaching to bridge the space between them.

'I'm sorry. Really...I am sorry. Last night and everything but___'

Bill took the hand and squeezed three fingers.

'Do you want me to come_____?' A word of sympathy was due.

'No.' She was even more insistent than before. 'You stay. I'll be okay. These things happen.'

'You sure?'

'Yes. It's your last night. What's to be gained from you coming back? I'll be okay.'

He felt fingers working their way along the length of his forearm. 'Honestly...I'll be fine.'

Circumstances demanded he'd settle the bill. She reached for her bag and minutes later was round his side of the table, leaning to meet him.

'Enjoy your night.' She kissed him once, twice and then a third time on the lips. He turned to return the kiss.

'Get back safely.'

'I'll try.'

She managed a smile. He watched her go, weaving in and out of chairs and with a final glance over her shoulder – disappear into the crowds lining the street.

He turned to his beer, a glass raised to the infamous dodgy prawn though he knew from experience these things were no laughing matter, particularly with them going home tomorrow. Carol too was sympathetic on returning to the scene to be put in the picture.

'Doesn't seem to have been her week one way or another,' she remarked.

Bill thought it best to say nothing.

All that remained – whether to head straight for the *German Bar* or stop-off somewhere en-route. Maybe on this occasion heading straight there would be the wise move. He didn't want to miss out on the last chance to be with Ava through getting his timing wrong. Ten minutes later he took his wallet from the table and checked he'd got everything.

The bar was as on previous visits, not too quiet whilst never getting to the point of people spilling onto the street. He ordered a large *Warsteiner* and took a newspaper to avoid drawing attention.

It was a third of the way down the glass that the newspaper was politely put to one side to be replaced by Ava's smiling face and seconds later, a kiss planted firmly on the lips.

'Hi...Remember me?'

'Hi.'

He watched her settle, the wave of hair swept from her face. Beer ordered they exchanged looks, seeing who'd be first to break the ice, updating each other on their day with likely some reference to the previous evening.

He wasn't sure about mentioning it. Whether it warranted a comment or would be perceived as being intrusive. That she might not welcome him grilling her about meeting her fellow countrymen in her own time at the bar. He didn't want to come across like some nerdy kid.

She saved him the trouble of agonising over it, shifting closer.

'I saw you last night.' The way she put it seemed to invite a reaction. 'I wasn't being nosey. But in a bar this size it isn't easy to avoid people totally.'

He was relieved she'd seen fit to mention it. His explanation ready at hand – that it was the way events had panned-out though not in the way he would have chosen.

Ava listened, but with little more to say on the subject. There were no grounds for it to be an issue. They gave quick resumes of their day. In her case, an unscheduled drive to Malaga to a clinic regarding some health issue with her uncle. It sounded strange to hear of her driving somewhere. For some reason she hadn't struck him as the car-driving sort, at least not here in Spain. Further evidence this was as much home as a holiday destination.

He filled her in on his day. The trip on the bus and wander round the city under Helen's tutored eye. Ava appeared interested but without pressing him on the details. She added a few bits on the history, Bill managing to recall a few details about rebuilding walls and towers. They got onto more recent history, touching on what little they knew of Franco's stint in charge: something Bill had noticed never appeared to be raised or mentioned in the cafes or bars, even, it appeared, between the Spaniards. Possibly too controversial a topic to warrant discussion in public places, or maybe just in the presence of foreigners. It brought further compliments on her English; compliments she was quick to brush aside.

He told her about the journey, how they passed time reading, especially Helen with her appetite for crime-novels, at times getting through close to a book a day on holiday. How she'd armed herself with a good half dozen volumes to keep her going. They talked about their own reading. Her preference, not surprisingly, German writers: Thomas Mann, Gunther Grass. Bill listened but without grasping the points entirely. It was often the case when it came to the heavier stuff – an area he was inclined to venture into with care though it wasn't always easy to say why. Other than finding some of it, if not most of it, a bit beyond him – even at times, difficult to follow. Or, if not *follow*, to have any real empathy with. Or maybe it was the intensity of feelings which he wasn't much given to dwelling on. By way of redressing the balance he told her how he rated *The Innocent* by Ian McEwan which coincidentally, was set in Germany. And *Kafka*. You were always on a safe bet with *Kafka*. Even if admitting to finding the middle bits of his stories a bit hard going.

She smiled, her attention switching to the more pressing matter of ordering more beers.

Both were aware of the time. Not just in terms of being in the bar but, in Bill's case, of it being his last hours in Spain if you discounted the start of the following day.

It was agreed to make the next one their last. Bill watched as Ava headed for the bar to place the order and to save time, settle the bill there and then. Trying not to spend too long admiring the smooth skin of her calves beneath the cut-off jeans, the streak of hair tossed from one shoulder to the other – stark reminders they were approaching the end of their time together.

On leaving the bar she immediately reached for his hand and then further, allowing an arm to encircle his back, Bill quick to follow suit.

Reaching the seafront they walked the slow climb along the path. On a night with minimum time to spare they quickly took their seats, heads resting on each other's shoulders before a quick exchange of kisses – the signal to make their descent to the grassy ledge that – on this occasion – was in near total darkness.

Out of necessity, their fucking would be distinctly functional, foreplay kept to a little kissing, a little fondling before positioning herself for what was, by now, a familiar position: confirmation she was still the one calling the shots.

Back on open ground they allowed themselves a minute or two on the bench. An opportunity to take stock of what had happened in what little time they'd had together. Reassurances that it had been good. That he mustn't be too hard on himself for allowing it to happen.

It was an unhappy parting from Bill's point of view. Physically he fancied Ava more than any woman he'd met. Admittedly it was largely sexual – the sight of her naked, the smoothness of her body, the small breasts, hair tossed back and forth: a show of complicity in what was happening. But it wasn't just that. There was a freshness, a vigour about her that was both comforting and reassuring to Bill. Particularly in light of the way things were between him and Helen. Aided by the way events had slotted so comfortably into place: Helen's early departures, Ava's arrivals in the *German Bar*. And that in a little over twelve hours' time he'd be boarding a plane without Helen having an inkling of what had happened.

Thoughts remaining with him as he climbed from the cab, tipped generously and for the last time, reached for the key.

However brief the time away there was the always that flat feeling when it came to an end: the rituals of homeward travel: departure-gates, tickets, passports.

To pass time they walked the length of Malaga airport's new space-age-look concourse: bars, restaurants, shops selling just about every hand-held electronic gadget the modern-day traveller could seek to accompany him on his trip home.

They settled for a coffee and a slice of almond cake at one of the huge open-plan cafes, but it would never rate alongside the café at The Balcon or in Friguana. Or any of the last few days' most memorable moments – or a large *Warsteiner* at the *German Bar*.

As they boarded the plane, Bill took a last glance at the backdrop of mountains cast in a haze of sunlight beneath a pale blue sky.

But before he'd had a chance to focus on bars and villas stretching in their shadow, they'd reached the porthole entry to the aircraft.

Post script.

Closing the patio door behind her, a slim legged figure dressed in cut-down shorts and a loose-fitting top stepped onto the balcony, pulling the white plastic chair from under the table. Though the midsummer temperatures were some way behind them it was still plenty warm enough to sit outside. Settling into place she opened the lid of her lab-top and pulled herself closer to the table whilst reaching for the mug of coffee. Drinking slowly she opened her first email.....

Hi Ava...You're honoured. The first social email, and definitely the longest I've sent in years (or ever). I hope you're well and in good spirits and that your uncle is in good health. I couldn't resist proving you wrong. You said I'd never get round to contacting you because I wasn't 'that sort of person'. Maybe you're right, but I'm doing it all the same. Anyway, enough of the waffle (English for nonsense!)

Hope you don't mind me sending this email, if only to say that meeting you in Spain was memorable, at least for me. And I'm not just talking about the end of the evenings (though that was pretty good too!)

You'll remember we talked about things back in England so I thought I'd update you on what's happened since we arrived back in the UK. It may be that at this stage you're not too interested and I wouldn't blame you for that. But I won't deny that one of the reasons for contacting you apart from letting you know what's happened is to say it would be fairly easy to pop over to Spain, even for the occasional weekend. Flights are cheaper out of season and it would be no hassle on my part. But....please don't think I'm talking about making it a regular occurrence. You have commitments and I would no way want to, or seek to, interfere with that.

But maybe I'm already getting ahead of myself (hope I'm not confusing you. Your English is so good I tend to forget it isn't your first language.) What I'm saying is...to get back to telling you what's happened since our return in the Summer.

Me and Helen split up not long after our return to the UK. It was no surprise to either of us and probably not to you either. I know I talked about some of the difficulties we were having.

But we're still on speaking terms and I think she's okay with that. We've met a couple of times since splitting up. And I remember you being interested when I talked about the problems between us being to do with the physical side (I'm guessing you know what I mean...the sex side.) I know you would have liked to know more but as I said at the time it would have been difficult with Helen still on the scene. But I can understand you asking about it. I think women are more inclined to show interest in these things than men, or than a lot of people give them credit for.

Anyway, the truth was, and I don't have any problem with you knowing this, Helen never really liked sex. In fact, she didn't like it at all. We slept together after a fashion but it never amounted to much. I'm hoping, from memory, you're okay with me talking like this. I remember – and I'm sure you do too – discussing people's attitudes to sex; how some people experiment whilst others just stick to what they know or maybe just don't want to talk about it. Or maybe – as on the case of Helen – don't bother at all!

Where her worries or anxieties about sex come from I don't know. We rarely talked about it. Only once I remember her talking about an incident with her mother in South Africa when she was very young that might have had something to do with it; some incident in a house that led to them having to escape in the middle of the night. She'd been pretty tearful telling me about it, and fairly drunk, and I didn't bother pressing her on the details. I just think something happened – something to do with men, possibly strangers – that probably made a huge impression.

Anyway, whatever the reason, she made her feelings on the subject clear on the first night we were together. I don't think I reacted at first. I thought it was probably to do with some bad experiences. That she'd been with a man, or men, who – when it comes to sex – wasn't too sensitive towards women.

Anyway, I think both me and Helen had known more or less from the start that the sex thing was never going to work long-term; that it was really only a matter of time before we went our separate ways.

I've met Helen a few times since we broke up and we talk a bit about what happened. She'd moved jobs, gone to work in Essex which is a county east of London. She told me she was going out with a man called Aadesh, or Desh as I think she called him, someone who worked in her department: an ex college teacher from Mumbai. A man she'd become friendly with after we'd finished. Or so she says, which may be true but I'm not entirely convinced. It seems a bit of a coincidence. She talked quite a bit about the guy when we met. How he was quite an ambitious bloke pushed a lot by his parents to be successful...whatever that's supposed to mean (possibly a cultural thing, if you follow me.) Anyway she talked about him being quite conservative in his thinking (in this case meaning a bit old fashioned and traditional...unlike me, or you as far as I can remember.) Which made me think that in a number of respects he may be a more suitable partner for her. Something she might have realised earlier than she was suggesting and might have prompted the idea of us finishing. She says she met him after we'd finished but to be honest I'm not that bothered. I can hardly claim innocence in such matters! I just hope they manage to make a go of it. She needs someone she can get on with in all senses.

From my point of view I haven't met anyone since we finished (honestly!) But I'm not too bothered and haven't yet got round to browsing dating-sites or anything like that! I've had the odd night out...we'll say no more.

But – and this is where I hope I'm not speaking out of turn, or sounding really corny – you remember we talked about that word. I really would like to see you again at some point, can I say sooner rather than later. Like I say, it's easy for me to get over to Malaga and then treat myself to a taxi to your place. If you're not keen and prefer to put what happened between us behind you, I can hardly blame you. But I would be disappointed. Sorry if I'm sounding corny but it's often difficult to put things differently.

At the very least I hope you'll reply to the email. Thanks for agreeing to give me the address.

I really do hope to see you again, but if not, I wish you all the best and thanks for everything.

Luv Bill XXX

She finished the coffee and looked beyond the balcony to where – on days such as this – a thin haze gave an impression of the whole coastline: sea, sun sky – cargo-ships en-route to goodness knows where – having come to a near standstill.

Her uncle would be expecting his lunchtime sandwich soon. But it could wait, she wasn't yet ready to shift herself back indoors. She scrolled down the screen, clicking an entry on a previous page.

She began reading...

Ava.....Hope you don't mind me contacting you like this but I couldn't let too many days pass without some communication.

A heartfelt thanks for everything. I can barely recall a problem in the whole four days and for that I thank you hugely. I know you're probably not overly interested in what's happening on our own shores but I thought you might like to know me and Bill finally went our separate ways shortly after returning from Spain. The break was fairly smooth, both of us aware it had been on the cards for a while (sorry, I hope you can follow this...that we both knew it would happen) if equally guilty of not stirring ourselves to do anything about it before.

But I have to say you played your part – in a good way. We parted on good terms; I think we both wanted it to happen but were prepared to leave to each other to make the final break. I always liked Bill. Loved him even, and in a way, I still do. Though maybe that sounds a bit corny (do you know the word 'corny'? – a bit like 'silly'). We started going out after I'd ended a relationship with a man called Gus, an Egyptian oddly enough. The son of a rich business man. He's the kind who likes to give the impression he's about to make big money, but without appearing to do much about making it happen. But for all that he was extremely generous and a very considerate person, and good company. Quite old fashioned in terms of relationships: sex – which was rarely mentioned – only ever raised in the context of producing children: a bit old-fashioned I know and not something I could agree with in principle, though in my case there were reasons for not making an issue out of it.

Which goes some way to explaining you arriving on the scene; the point being – I know I never got round to explaining this: something of the background as to what happened between me and Bill which led to me contacting you. Fact is, and it sounds strange to hear me saying it...I've never been into sex. I know it raises a few eyebrows (sorry, I keep using these expressions but take it as a compliment. Your English seems so good in your emails I sometimes forget you're German. 'Raising eyebrows' is saying something odd; apologies if you knew that.) And I have to say it's much easier talking about these things to another female. I hope you don't mind and can put up with me a little longer. But when you feel the way I do about such things you can sometimes feel cut off and – as I often do...guilty. Which was always the root of the problem with Bill.

I knew it was only fair to put him in the picture fairly early. On the first night together as I remember, and he actually took it well, though I wasn't too surprised. I've been in similar situations before and my guess is most men don't fully believe what I'm saying; not that I'm lying, but that it's to do with some problem that will eventually go away, that I'll recover from, like some illness. Which I think was the case with Bill, not so much an 'illness' but that he hoped, or expected at some point I'd come round and everything would be okay – one of the reasons we stayed together as long as we did...two and a half years.

Why I feel the way I do about sex is difficult to say and probably not something you'd want me to bore you with. Put briefly – I wish I could give a nice easy answer. All I know is though I like to be close to a partner, the sex bit doesn't feel right to me; like there's too much demanded of me – physical or otherwise. Whether it's partly hereditary (passed down by parents) or stemming from something in the past, I don't know. The only thing I can link it to is something involving my mother when we were living in South Africa when I was very young, maybe two or three. There was a night there'd been a lot of people in the house, I don't know why, and we were in a crowded room, and at some point there were screams and though I have no knowledge of it, I was pulled to my feet and dragged away. Something to this day my mum flatly refuses to talk about. Exactly what happened I don't know; I've never been told. But I have an impression of us frequently needing to move house. I'm fairly sure my mother bears some guilt, or so my father put to me many years later when I was a near-adult, like even at that age it was to do with stuff I'd be better off not knowing about. I know I'm going on a bit but it isn't the kind of thing I'd have felt comfortable talking about with Bill. I think I only mentioned it once. They say the adult is formed in the first five years of her life and maybe there's something from that time that's still around. But you can never be sure and it's easy and tempting to try to find ready explanations for these things. And to be honest I don't even think about it much now.

But all the time I was with Bill I felt awkward, not so much guilty but knowing I was denying him something most couples take for granted. Plus, I didn't want my relationship with him to end, at least not yet. So we came to a kind of compromise where I'd kind of help him out sexually, if you get what I'm hinting at – but perhaps that's enough said about that.

For me things changed when I started a new job in a smaller town about thirty miles from London. I had an apprentice assigned to me. An Indian chap by the name of Aadesh who'd worked as a teacher in Mumbai and had come to the UK with the blessing of his parents. He knew about Bill and though far from wanting to be seen breaking up relationships I think he got the idea all wasn't brilliant between us, and if he had his way things would be different. We'd talked about relationships in the general sense. How he'd been serious with two women though neither had come to anything, one I think was to do with the class – or caste thing – which still seems to be a big deal in India.

What I did know was I was getting a clear message from him; that he was looking for a serious relationship, whilst giving the impression it had little to do with any physical aspect, which also had me listening. It was clearly down to me to make a decision and pretty quickly. And given the way things were between me and Bill I knew it was the time to make it.

The whole idea of dating-sites couldn't – at first – have been further from my mind. I'd been chatting with a friend at work, Phyll, who was talking about it and admitted she'd been a party to that kind of thing on a number of occasions. Which wasn't – and isn't – in any way putting it down. I now see they serve a purpose that makes sense, maybe more sense than going through the process of meeting someone in a bar or club. Or as in my case, at work.

It was after work one afternoon that she scrolled through a few sites, just by way of passing time. I was intrigued when she went a bit further onto a different page and scrolled down to something called 'Foreign Fields' with Spain mentioned. Telling her I'd been to Spain she clicked on one or two and it was then that I saw your ad. In the place we'd been to last year.

At the time I didn't think much more about it – but it was later, on the way home thinking about what I'd seen and the whole business of me and Bill, and meeting people that way, that the idea occurred. Which was the day before I first made contact with you.

Even now I'm not sure whether I ought to feel guilty. I know it was a deceitful (dishonest) move, particularly in light of what was involved: flights accommodation...everything, and the 'birthday idea' was a useful cover-up. But it had to be that way if it was to work out the way I'd planned. And the thing I couldn't get out of my head was not so much that I owed him what I was doing, but that it seemed a way of making up for something that, since we'd met, he'd been denied. A reward for his patience though it really sounds bad putting it that way. Also with Aadesh having appeared on the scene, I can't deny it was a little test put his way to see how he'd react. Plus – it was his birthday!

I hope you're okay with everything I'm saying here. I don't want you to feel you were being used in a way you wouldn't want. What would happen between you and Bill I had no problem with, otherwise I would never have gone ahead with it.

And I have to say you played your part brilliantly. I know we'd sorted all the details beforehand: the times, the bar he'd almost certainly head for with me off the scene. But with anyone else I'm not sure it would have worked anything like as well. And for that – a huge thanks. Thanks incidentally for agreeing to sort these things by email, it made things a lot easier.

Looking back I'm happy that the whole thing went so smoothly. I'm pretty sure he was really fond of you too, which doesn't surprise me. I certainly know he has, or had, a thing about 'petite' women that was in the description next to your ad.

Once we we'd got to Spain things went more or less as I'd planned. The leaving early because of the drink, the 'illness' following a pizza were handy (convenient) excuses. Hope you don't mind me appearing on the scene one of the nights, as we'd arranged. I couldn't resist the temptation of meeting you face to face if only briefly at the bar.

Plus, I couldn't resist a few other moments: the odd word of German, particularly 'auf wiedersehen' in Friguana and asking if he'd met anyone. I was just interested to see how he'd deal with it. And later in the German Bar. A little 'goodbye' as we were leaving but with Bill clearly in mind. I dropped a few other topics into the conversation: a bit about my family, knowing how he feels about my dad who's about as different from Bill as it gets.

But it's behind us now – in all senses. Aadesh is a different soul altogether and I'm happy with him. But I look back on some good times with Bill, particularly the four days in Spain which were memorable in a number of respects. I don't know if or when I'll get out to Spain again but I thank you again for the part you played. And again, I hope you don't mind me talking at such length. But I feel we got to know each other to some extent in our exchanges beforehand and if I'm ever in Spain again I'd be happy to meet up one night. Again, many thanks and very best wishes,

Yours affectionately, Helen Ormrod.

She stared at the screen a moment longer, thinking there might be signs of movement inside. She got up to look. Her uncle was dozing as he'd got in the habit of doing at this time of day. Which was fine; best to leave him a while.

She was back to her computer, scrolling back up the page, clicking a more recent addition to the *inbox...*

A man in Barcelona, twenty-five years of age, dark hair and of medium build who'd be visiting the area shortly and would like to meet with her....

Placing the cup on the table to one side, she began typing.

* * * * *

Two For The Road

The idea occurred to Sammy whilst seated on his customary spot at the foot of the drive-in to Mac's Burger-Joint – a favourite spot of his on the fringe of town. A place where a man could relax and be himself a while. In Sammy's case an opportunity to be seized with both arms.

Born some months before his allotted time and semi-invalided at the age of three on account of being struck by a car swerving to avoid a cat running into the road – Sammy's start in life had been far from ideal. But as his elders and mentors: teachers, nurses, preachers – not to mention his ma...had been at pains to point out: these things happen and at such an age the body has a knack of adapting to these things. That there'd be every chance of getting himself around just so long as he made full use of the bits still in working order. Plus – there was little to be gained from whingeing about circumstances that were, after all, beyond his control. What he needed to do was to get himself back on his feet, dust himself down and set about making the most of whatever opportunities happened to come his way.

Which – on the day in question – was what drew his attention to a figure plodding his way up the path heading for Mac's Burger-Joint. A huge man built like an ox but treading in a series of short hesitant steps: a man either extremely short-sighted or more likely still – devoid of sight altogether.

Enough to have Sammy sit up and watch more closely.

A little thought was required, but if – as he suspected – this was just another guy drifting off the highway with a little time on his hands – an idea was stirring that could lead to a little luck heading *both* their ways.

In light of which he made his move: rotating on his elbows to launch himself into his established method of getting around: using his arms and elbows as a lever and his legs as a kind of rudder. Three or four minutes lapsing before drawing himself alongside the spot where the man was stood aside the hatch eating a burger and passing time with Mac.

Introducing himself he shuffled into position, his legs folded beneath him in his customary seated pose.

The man – whose name was Billy – looked in the direction of the voice, but was saying nothing. People approaching out of the blue were routinely regarded as what his mother would term *mischief makers*: folk intent on fleecing people like Billy – the unfortunate folk of the world – for every dime in their pocket, and for no good reason other than fleecing unfortunate folk was deemed to be a justified way of making a few bucks without call to be busting a gut to get it.

Himself no stranger to being accosted in public – Sammy knew the way to get to people like Billy, ie. people who – like himself – had been handed a bum deal in life for no good reason, was to waste no time in getting down to business.

Drawing alongside Billy he gave him the lowdown on his own stroke of misfortune: explaining how – curtesy of an air-head motorist – his legs had got mashed when he was a kid and how he got around by shuffling along on his elbows using his legs as a kind of rudder.

Billy was listening but only vaguely. A hard-luck tale amounting to a little trouble getting around was hardly going to get much sympathy...or money, from a guy without the benefit of sight – mashed legs or no mashed-up legs.

But being nothing if not patient – and persistent – Sammy shuffled closer, looking left and then right before putting Billy in the picture as to a plan he'd been he'd been hatching whilst observing his arrival on the scene some ten minutes ago.

In short – Billy – who was built like an ox but couldn't see, would take Sammy – who was as light as a stack of bones but couldn't walk...on his back whenever they stepped outside; in effect – Sammy being the *eyes* whilst Billy would provide the *legs* – the pair able to help each other out in a way that to this point, neither would have thought feasible.

Billy was saying nothing. Talk was cheap and stuff about 'helping each other out' was hardly music to his ears. Aside from which, he didn't know the guy. Who was to say he wasn't just another hoodlum drifting in off the street intent on ripping him off at the earliest opportunity, only to disappear as and when the mood took him?

Which – to the casual observer – was certainly a possibility. Whilst Sammy might point out that Billy, being by far the stronger of the two, could take any opportunity *he* liked to beat Sammy to a pulp, take what little money he carried and leave him for dead in the street – as and when the mood took him.

Though inclined to greet all advice, suggestions, offers of *a better life* with a degree of scepticism, Billy was no fool, aware that – like it or not – people in his position ultimately depended on the good will of others to get by; sometimes to the extent of getting from A to B and living to tell the tale. And though at first glance the idea sounded pretty far-out, if not completely dumb – there *was* a kind of logic in what the guy was saying: grounds for maybe giving it a little further thought.

He turned to Mac, the owner of the burger stand who – on acknowledging Billy's signal – led him to the rear of the caravan where he could fill Billy in on what he knew of Sammy. Able to confirm that he'd seen him on a number of occasions – usually seated in the same spot at the end of the drive-in, minding his own business and generally coming across as an okay guy 'cept for problems he had getting around..

Billy listened, eventually returning to the front of the caravan where Sammy had barely shifted. And on hearing Billy's announcement – that on giving it some thought and on the advice of his friend Mac, he would go along with Sammy's plan, but – on the strict understanding that at the first hint of mischief he'd be off and that would be the end of it...

Sammy was instantly up on his elbows, inviting Billy to join him to get a few details sorted. First and foremost deciding which of the pair's apartments would be best suited for them to hang out in.

It was agreed that Sammy's place would be the better option. A ground floor apartment with mod-cons, a spare room and a decent sized garden.

They also needed to come to an arrangement as to how they'd organise things, needing to work together but also recognising the need not to be crowding each other's space. In effect – a 'marriage' of convenience with little attempt or desire to live out of each other's pockets.

Having got that much clear it was time to start putting theory into practice. First stop – Billy's place to get a few bits and bobs together and a change of clothes.

But before that – a chance to put the basic idea to the test: Sammy climbing aboard Billy's back, arms hooked round his shoulders, his legs left dangling either side of Billy's hips. The whole performance witnessed by Mac, as intrigued as he was amused to see the pair take their first tentative steps toward the road to take them in the direction of town.

Bearing Sammy on his back proved to be no big deal, no greater burden than carrying his weekly groceries. And with Sammy's arms gripped tight round Billy's neck, he was ideally placed to see left and right over Billy's shoulder and give precise instructions as to the pace and direction of movement.

As might be expected they were the focus of considerable attention. Some assuming Sammy was the victim in a road accident or a disabled relative in need of hospital attention. Kids pointed from the rear seats of cars, nagging their parents to stop a while to share a joke or hand them a stick of candy.

But the pair knew to remain focused on the task in hand and once settled into a kind of routine – halfway between a trot and a jog – progress was considerable: a little over an hour seeing them arrive at Billy's apartment where, under Sammy's watchful eye, he was able to gather a few belongings in a bag to be tied round his waist or slung over his shoulder before setting off on the next lap to Sammy's place to start getting things sorted there – arms again clasped round his neck, legs drawn in slightly but not so as to impede Billy's stride or worse still, trip him up and have the pair plummet to the ground.

On arrival at Sammy's place, they set about getting Billy's room into some kind of shape – a few clothes stuffed in drawers, bedding fished out of a cupboard. Leaving what remained of the day to do a bit of exploring and take advantage of a situation that a few hours ago would have been little more than a far-fetched pipedream.

But first things first. Before that – a little shopping. Chance to put their combined effort into something beyond the relatively straightforward business of getting from A to B.

They caused quite a stir in the hyper-market. Shoppers taking time out from loading their baskets and trolleys to take in the spectacle of Billy pushing a trolley, Sammy perched on his back, leaning to lift packets and tins and dump them into the trolley.

It was agreed they'd get the stuff back to Sammy's before heading elsewhere though there was some discussion as to how best to carry the two bags; Sammy hooking one over each shoulder proving the most practical solution.

With the groceries dumped it was off to the local park. A moment that seemed to define where they were at in light of what was essentially a new beginning for the pair of them: the ducks, the flowers, the lake with its flotilla of boats, the ice-cream man in his wagon…all coming under the radar in a way several hours ago neither could possibly have envisaged.

Back at Sammy's place they worked on what was to become a daily routine: Sammy dealing with stuff at ground level, Billy sorting out stuff on work-tops – tidying, washing, taking stuff from cupboards and cooking under Sammy's watchful eye.

Their evenings – if largely uneventful – were pleasant enough: mostly spent watching tv: baseball and gymnastics taking pride of place. The pair delighting in watching guys do stuff they were barely able to contemplate, Billy getting a running commentary from Sammy so he didn't miss out too much on what was going on.

It was as Spring gave way to Summer that Sammy suggested they take a trip out to Mac's place. Chance to say 'hi' to an old acquaintance and re-visit the spot where their little arrangement had been conceived. There'd be no argument from Billy. In the past Mac had always looked out for him, dishing out free burgers from time to time and helping him get the right bus back to town at the end of his visits.

It was the following Wednesday that they doubled-up to set off and see how their old buddy was faring – an extra jaunt in their step at the prospect of re-living the moment when it had all begun.

Mac was quick to greet them and pleased to hear how well things had worked out. Billy happy to admit – in a quiet moment whilst Sammy was returning to the spot where he'd first spotted Billy – just how his life had been turned around. Prepared to concede that his initial scepticism – if understandable at the time – had proved quite unwarranted.

It was on leaving the pair in conversation that Sammy – scuttling along a bit of path to a spot he remembered well – came across a figure perched on the grass close to where he was heading: a girl sitting on her haunches picking petals from a flower and tossing them into the breeze.

On venturing closer he could see she was a real cutey, with the bluest eyes and the blondest hair you ever saw. The kind of girl many a man would happily die for.

Shuffling along on his elbows he reached the spot where the girl continued to pick bits of the flower and launch them into the air on a count of one to five.

Aware of someone approaching she stopped and looked up. 'Hi,' she said.

Sammy returned the greeting. 'Hi. How you doin'?'

'I'm doin' good,' the girl said, stressing the 'good' in the over-the-top way girls were apt to do.

'Good.' Sammy watched the bits of flower being discarded with a flick of exceptionally nimble fingers.

Whatever he had in mind – and he wasn't entirely sure what it was he *did* have in mind, he knew that girls of the kind he was talking to needed to be approached with caution; in the case of folk like Sammy – with a good deal of caution. And that a little cajolery might be required in order to get her attention.

On introducing herself, the girl – whose name was Suzy – made a show of listening whilst continuing to pick at the flower – and keep an eye on proceedings by Mac's caravan where a hunk of a guy built like an ox was stood chatting to the man at the counter.

Sammy had adopted his customary pose to set about putting Suzy in the picture – being born some time before his allotted slot and getting mashed at the age of three by a car swerving to avoid a cat running into the road – a combination of which meant getting around on his elbows using his legs as a kind of rudder.

Suzy picked the last petal off the stalk and launched it into the sky. She was kind of listening but finding it hard to picture. Getting born early and then mashed by a car at the age of three didn't sound like fun. Certainly not as much fun as spending time with the hunk of a guy still stood at the counter and who she liked to think was taking every opportunity to look in her direction.

'Who's the big guy?' she asked, unable to keep her curiosity in check any longer.

Sammy looked to where Billy was still chatting to Mac.

'That's Billy,' he said. 'Sad case. Can't see nothing.'

Suzy peered in the direction of the caravan, straining to get a closer look.

'Gee...that's bad. I can't imagine not being able to see nothing.'

Continuing to curl strings of grass through her fingers, she set about telling Sammy her tale – or the bit that had sprung to mind whilst picking the last few petals off the stalk....

How she was really just an ordinary little girl who, ever since being in her high chair, had a weakness for flowers, particularly big pink flowers the like of which she'd spotted in the adjacent field on her arrival only half an hour ago, and which she'd been so stupid as to walk past without stopping to pick a few. And if only someone would be so kind as to go back and pick some for her, she'd be so grateful that absolutely anything would be possible on their return...

Sammy looked to where a long wooden fence separated the field from its surroundings. A fence no more than a few feet high. A quick calculation telling him he'd be able to negotiate the fence, possibly by wriggling between the slats as opposed to clambering over it. And that once over it, picking a few flowers would be child's play so long as the grass wasn't so thick as to hinder his movements.

With an instruction to stick around and a promise he'd be back before she'd had time to blink – he did an about turn, scuttling off in the direction of the fence.

Suzy watched, waiting for him to reach the bit of road where the fence ran alongside the field before making her move – turning her attention to the caravan where the man built like an ox was stood munching a hot-dog and chatting to the café owner.

Getting herself to her feet she skipped along the grass verge, drawing level with the caravan and propping a leg against its wheel.

'Hi.'

Billy turned at the sound of the voice, instantly aware it didn't belong to Sammy.

'How you doin'?' she asked, for the first time viewing Billy's impressive features head-on.

'Okay,' said Billy – as ever, resolved to giving nothing away to folk springing up on him out of the blue.

'You're cute,' Suzy said, rolling her eyes and wearing a broad smile. 'Real cute…'

Billy looked at Mac who looked him briefly in the eye and then made a point of retreating into his caravan.

Finding herself alone with Billy was a plus – but also a reminder of the need to move quickly.

'I got an idea,' she said, her leg crooked higher, her voice dropping to a whisper as she set about putting Billy in the picture as to the idea she'd had whilst sitting a few yards down the road and spotting Billy in conversation with Mac…

That Billy would take Suzy – who, by comparison, weighed very little – on his back, for her to be his 'eyes' and in return, she would be…'his girl', happy to do absolutely anything for him and pander to him in whatever way sprang to mind!

Billy looked in the direction the offer was coming from but, for now at least, was saying nothing.

'I'm cute…some say *real* cute!' Suzy said. 'I got blue eyes and long blonde hair – and the cutest little nose you ever saw on a girl…or *imagined* you ever saw on a girl,` she added quickly, remembering too late that the man couldn't see a darned thing.

Billy was intrigued, but at the same time, reminded of yet another of his mother's warnings: that females fitting Suzy's description were invariably just another breed of *mischief makers* – in this case for reasons that would become apparent as he got a little older. But in the meantime – to no way entertain or encourage them. In fact, best move of all – give them as wide a berth as possible and keep his mouth shut.

For Billy it was more straightforward, in that when it came to folks' appearances; be it blonde-haired dames, blue-eyed dames: good-looking, not-so-good-looking or even plain ugly: each was one and the same to him; none likely to have him going head over heels in any direction.

Plus – there was Sammy to consider. A guy who'd become as much a friend as an accomplice and who deserved better than to be dumped as and when the first opportunity arose.

And so, it was, with regret that Billy declined Suzy's offer, explaining how he and Sammy – the guy she might have spotted on his back earlier – had already come to an arrangement along similar lines to what she had suggested.

Suzy looked dejectedly in the direction of the highway and adjacent field.

'Gee...that's too bad,' she said, putting both feet on the ground rearranging her skirt accordingly. 'Mind you... there's stuff I can do, a guy can never do.' She twirled a stalk of grass and lifted her leg back onto Mac's wheel.

Billy got the message but was not given to compromising himself; not even in such circumstances as the girl was clearly hinting at.

Suzy too got the message. And was quick to recall the advice of *her* mother: that looking cute was fine, and as a blonde-haired, blue-eyed female she'd always have the edge when it came to getting a man's attention. But that there are times when it pays to be a good deal cuter than you look if you really wanted to take advantage of whatever opportunities happened to come your way.

'Okay,' Suzy said. 'I get what you're saying...but___'

She stood a moment, working on how best to put another plan she'd just been hatching into operation.

'I got a bit of a problem.' As she spoke her eye drifted to the traffic heading back and forth along the highway.

Billy listened as Suzy went on to explain how her mom had got sick and with the bus back to town being due in no more than twenty minutes if he could give her a lift as far as the bus stop she'd be real grateful and do anything to repay him. The point being that he could get her there so much quicker. And both knew the highway was no place for a girl on her own with all the cars passing and drivers calling all kind of stuff through the windows.

She paused to let it be known how sore she was at having to ask this kind of favour. 'It's just...you know; if anything was the happen to my mom____'

Billy knew about moms. He knew about buses too and looked again in the direction the girl was indicating. Maybe there was something in what she was saying, maybe not. But he guessed there'd be no harm in giving her a few moments of his time. It wouldn't be for long and there was no sign of Sammy putting in an appearance just yet. And for all his mom's warnings Suzy hardly seemed the type to stab him in the back the minute she got the opportunity.

He shook himself down and arched his back as invitation for her to climb aboard.

'Gee thanks.'

Within seconds her arms were clasped round his neck, her legs – bared from the thigh down – dangling one each side of Billy's hips. 'Let's go...!'

With little to choose between Suzy and Sammy in terms of weight, they were quickly into their stride, Billy following her directions that took them down the drive-in to the highway, or rather, alongside the highway where Suzy signalled a right turn keeping them out of harm's way along the grass verge.

'This is fun!' Suzy squealed as they hit the tarmac, an arm waved at the occupants of passing cars whose offers of assistance went well beyond anything Billy was in a position to provide.

Though the grass was proving a bit of a problem, Sammy had been able to gather a fair number of flowers. The only problem was carrying them. Shuffling through a field on his elbows was tricky enough but carrying a fistful of flowers meant folding an arm at the elbow and levering himself through the grass, leaving the other hand to hold the flowers out of harm's way.

It was on picking something like his twentieth flower that he was distracted by a high pitched squealing noise from somewhere over by the road.

He looked up in time to see a mane of yellow hair and someone or something beneath racing along as if taking part in some kind of charity run.

'Hi...!' Her eyes glued on the field, Suzy waved at the sight of Sammy's head poking above a sea of grass.

Though there was something vaguely familiar about the voice his view was hindered and he wasn't yet done picking the flowers. And the longer he delayed, the less time he'd have to reap the rewards on his return. He was quickly back to work, crawling on his elbow and picking the next flower from its stalk.

Back at the caravan Mac had emerged from temporary hiding. Whilst more than happy to dish out what advice he could to the likes of Sammy and Billy, he knew there were times to keep his distance. That a man's private life was his own business. And that whatever 'arrangement' Billy might have been about to come to with the likes of Suzy appearing on the scene, it would have nothing to do with him. His best move being to remove himself from the scene so as not to witness events first hand. The only logical conclusion being that Billy and the blonde chick were likely already half way to town in pursuit of a new life together.

It was as he was in the process of tidying up and contemplating an early closure that he spotted someone – or something – clambering between the slats of a fence at the end of the drive-in. A figure shuffling along on his elbow clutching what appeared to be a pink parasol under his other arm. A figure, on drawing closer, instantly identifiable as Sammy. With what he'd taken to be a pink parasol proving to be a bunch of flowers held aloft so as not to have them come into contact with the floor.

Mac sighed, wondering how best to deal with a situation he'd prefer not to have anything to do with.

Sammy was just glad to be back. He'd almost lost the knack of getting around on his elbows and was thinking getting aboard someone's back again – be it Suzy's or Billy's – couldn't come soon enough.

Which raised the whole issue of Billy. Something he'd given a little thought to whilst dragging himself back and forth across the field. Quite how he was going to manage that little conundrum remained to be seen. But the fact was opportunities to get a little action with the likes of Suzy didn't come round too often, especially when you were born premature and got around on your elbows using your legs as a kind of rudder. And what Billy needed to bear in mind was that they had come to an agreement; that their relationship was one of convenience so as not to be seen crowding each other's space.

He looked left and right – spotting no-one except Mac leaning on the counter looking a little edgy. He shuffled closer, putting the bouquet of flowers to one side.

'Hi there.'

Mac continued to lean on the counter as Sammy continued to look for signs of activity.

'Seen Suzy?'

'Suzy?'

'Yeh – the chick with the blonde hair and blue eyes who was sitting on the grass verge just down the road.'

Mac looked left and right for indication she might be somewhere in the vicinity.

'Can't say as I have.'

'Or how about Billy?' Sammy was on his elbows peering under the caravan to see if Billy was round the other side or playing some stupid game. He dragged himself back to the counter and took hold of the flowers.

Whatever his feelings about getting involved in other folks' business, Mac took little joy from seeing a guy crawling back and forth on his elbows not knowing which way to turn when he was able to step in and put him out of his misery. That when it came to women – the one thing guaranteed to make things worse was trying to kid a man there was a way of making them better.

'He's gone,' Mac said.

'Huh?'

'Gone...vanished!'

'What do you mean...vanished? Vanished where?'

'Dunno. He didn't say. That's what I mean by *vanished*.'

Mac turned to the fridge and took two burgers from the shelf.

'You hungry?' He slapped the burgers on the stove and tipped a few onion rings each side. After which he turned to Sammy, two hands slapped firmly on the counter.

'Billy – and the blonde kid – went off...together. Okay? End of story.'

There was the sound of cursing coupled with a disconsolate look both directions from Sammy, legs folded beneath him in his customary seated pose. A few minutes lapsing before hauling himself to the counter and taking hold of the flowers.

'Here...find a home for these,' he said.

'Onions?' Mac scooped the burger and reached for a bread roll.

'Forget it,' said Sammy. There was thinking to be done and decisions to be made. First of which was getting himself back to town to start clearing Billy's odds and ends from his room.

Mac watched as Sammy swivelled on his elbows and seconds later began scurrying at a rate of knots towards the tarmac.

On approaching the bus stop Billy had dumped Suzy off his back and was looking to be getting back before Sammy and Mac would be wondering what was going on and maybe getting worried. But Suzy was insistent that – with the bus being late, by at least twenty minutes [she must have got her times confused] – she buy Billy a soda or an ice-cream at the kiosk close by.

'Ten minutes ain't gonna make no difference. And a café or an ice-cream kiosk by a highway's no place for a girl to be seen on her own.'

Billy wasn't so sure. He'd been away a while and he didn't want to be seen as in any way taking advantage of people, especially Sammy who'd likely be looking at his watch wondering when they'd get to be heading off back to town.

'Okay…but only ten minutes,' he said.

Mac had finished cleaning the counter and was in the process of putting stuff away for the second time when his attention was once again drawn to a figure fumbling his way along the drive-in staggering from tree to tree in a series of short hesitant steps.

Eyes raised, he quickly turned away to tend to a few things beneath the counter – reminding himself that whatever was going on with these guys, it was nothing to do with him; that his job was to dish out coffee and burgers – nothing more, nothing less.

On saying his 'goodbyes' to Suzy [that took a little longer than he'd ben bargaining on] Billy was grateful to find himself back on familiar ground.

'Hi.'

Arriving at the hatch he turned to the area in and around the caravan.

Having had chance to catch his breath and with still no indication of Sammy anywhere in the vicinity he guessed he might just as well grab himself something to eat. Schlepping Suzy to the bus-stop had been an ordeal and a good deal further than she'd intimated. And without indication of any bus about to appear on the scene, he'd eventually made a rapid exit in order to get back to Mac's place.

'Been far?' Mac asked, watching Billy to see what reaction it got.

Billy wasn't sure how far he'd gone, except it had been far enough.

'Could say that,' he said, still searching for signs of Sammy. 'Been doin` a girl a favor....'

Mac was back below the counter taking a few plates from the bowl. He knew that *favors* of the kind Billy was referring to were apt to come in all shapes and sizes...like waiting for a guy to go picking flowers before moving in to whip his girl from under his nose. He drew himself back to full height.

'Sammy's gone,' he said, in a voice by this stage holding nothing back when it came to showing a little impatience.

'Huh?'

'Gone...vanished!'

'What do you mean vanished? Vanished where?'

'Dunno...didn't say. That's what I mean by *vanished*.'

'Which way'd he go?'

Mac turned in the direction Sammy had been heading.

'That way,' he said.

Billy was trying to guess what way *that way* was likely to be, something in Mac's voice suggesting it might not be wise to press him too far on the issue.

He sighed. It had been a long day and he was hardly in the mood for explanations.

The only consolation – a chance to catch his breath and reflect on the times he'd stood on this very spot without so much as a care in the world. And that were he to go back no more than six months in time, nothing would have changed.

'Hungry?' It was Mac's voice interrupting his thoughts.

'Why not?' Billy said. There was thinking to be done and decisions to be made. But they could wait a while.

'On the house,' said Mac, ladling a few onions and handing the burger to Billy's outstretched hand.

It was as Billy was taking the burger from Mac and figuring whether getting a cab would be his best move or maybe have Mac see him to the bus stop like in the old days – that a figure was to be seen skipping along the drive-in from the highway.

The voice was a familiar one, arriving before its owner had joined Billy at the counter.

Mac was already off the scene.

'Hi,' said a familiar voice. 'You'll never guess....'

Billy caught the voice but at that moment was beyond the point of guessing, or worrying too much about what she – or anyone – was at the point of saying.

Suzy looked to the ground.

'They gone and cancelled the bus and now there ain't no way I can get to my mom.'

She moved closer, a foot raised on the wheel, taking a firm grip on Billy's hand.

'It sure would be swell if you could help me out. I mean if you was to take me all the way to my mom...I could still be your eyes and do anything you want me to long after I've been to see her. I mean – there ain't no rush. We got all the time in the world. I could_____'

Billy stopped her right there.

'Don't you worry,' he said, a raised finger eventually settling on the tiny button of her nose. 'We'll get you to your mom.'

'Gee...thanks.'

Seconds later Billy was in position, arching his back as invitation for her to climb aboard.

'Okay...let's go,' Suzy cried, an arm waved at Mac who'd reappeared holding something aloft in a takeaway bag.

'You forgot your burger,' he was shouting after them.

* * * * *

Apes One To Four

The family making their way along the aisle stopped briefly at the pasta and rice shelf to take a packet of long-grain rice and add it to their trolley. A small detour followed allowing two packets of Bakewell Slices to be lifted from the shelf and placed next to the milk and potatoes before heading for the nearest cash-till without too long a queue, taking their place behind an elderly woman at the point of completing her purchase.

The girl on the till – a teenager wearing heavy make-up and a blue uniform – held the last of the customer's purchases against a screen and placed it next to a pack of fish-fingers.

'Twenty-four pounds forty.' She made it like an announcement, reminiscent of a bingo-caller approaching the end of her stint, looking to see how her friend and colleague Michelle was faring waiting for help with a product failing to register on her machine.

Back to her own till she handed the change and turned to the next batch of goodies, lifting each from its place on the conveyor belt, holding its bar-code to a screen and placing it on the 'done' side to be placed into bags.

The youngest members of the family were staring hard at the girl, following each packet and tin's progress from hand to screen to its new-found home in the bag handled by their father at the head of the queue: eyes staring sufficiently to have the girl wonder if there was something wrong with her – or the way she was handling the groceries.

The head of the family took a second bag and shook it a few times to begin loading more items one by one, the mechanical lifting of each item continuing to come under close scrutiny from the second youngest in the line, likely female though it was difficult to be absolutely sure.

But enough to distract the girl from the box of tea-bags to address the face of the second adult in the line, the one she assumed was the mother.

'You Apes?'

The figure she was addressing – Ape Two – nodded and lifted the last item into the bag before turning to her purse. Five bags of bananas followed the tea-bags into the canvas bag.

'We don't get many Apes,' the girl said, handling the final item, checking the total due and turning once again to Ape-Two.

'Twenty-four pounds, twenty-seven pence please.'

The father – Ape One – stepped in, dipping a hand into a bum-belt to retrieve a wallet.

'Have you got a *Loyalty Card*?' The question put like it was the thousandth time it had been asked within the hour.

Apes One and Two shook their heads. Dad replaced his wallet and turned to Ape-Two, signaling for her to follow him whilst making sure the kids were in-tow.

'Thankyou.' The girl waited for them to head for the door before looking to where her friend had resumed registering her customer's items on her machine.

'See them Mich..? She called across the space between the two tills. 'They was Apes!'

Her friend nodded, taking the next item from the belt and raising it to the screen.

'I thought they looked a bit weird.'

Both girls looked to where, seconds later, Apes One to Four disappeared through the automatic door.

'Cute ain't they, the little ones?' Her friend nodded, turning to the next batch of groceries sitting on the conveyor belt.

Back on the street the four were quick to fall into a military formation, making their way past the Coop and a number of other shops to the lights where they stopped waiting for the green-man signal to cross.

Looks were exchanged. Children – particularly younger children – intrigued to see what appeared to be a family of Apes, two carrying shopping, all four waiting for a little green man to allow them to cross the road.

'They Apes?' They would ask, the question put to the adults accompanying them, who looked briefly in the direction they were looking and nodded.

'I think so dear. Come on, we need to be getting back home.'

To the more elderly population who'd seen and lived through a lot in their lives, a family of Apes making their way down the street wasn't so much a big deal. They weren't the first visitors to arrive on their doorstep and were unlikely to be the last.

Though where they'd come from was the question on many people's lips a few days later. Most assuming it was from abroad. To the best of their knowledge apes didn't exist in the UK outside of zoos or theme parks. Probably Africa, or maybe South America. Which raised the question of how they'd come to arrive on these shores. Flown? Stowed away on a boat? Swam?

Possibly all three. Though since their arrival – first spotted from a sea-front late one afternoon – the second question was *why* they were here. Why a family of Apes would seek residency, temporary or otherwise, in a small coastal town in the UK.

It was some three weeks previous that they'd first been spotted; a young couple peering over the promenade rail at a scene of sunbathers and on glancing to their left, spotting a group apparently emerging from a dip in the sea, bearing haversacks, to occupy a spot behind a groyne: a group who – on closer examination – were seen not to be people at all, but a line of Apes. The pair, on exchanging glances, quick to take it upon themselves to inform the police without further delay.

A handful of uniformed officers arrived minutes later to confirm that the message they'd received over their radio wasn't 'bollocks' and that they were about to question a group of four Apes currently crouched behind a wall on the beach.

Standing in a line behind the promenade rail, they looked down and exchanged glances, the most senior amongst them calling from a distance. 'You Apes?'

The closest – Ape One, the one presumed to be the father – looked up and nodded before turning to his children, ushering them to keep close and not to say anything. He'd take it upon himself to deal with whatever questions were forthcoming.

Venturing onto the beach, the officers approached the group, pepper-sprays at hand. A few details were exchanged – an attempt to establish the circumstances that had brought a family of Apes to a small coastal town in the UK.

Pressing them proved a far from easy task, the Ape-Talk not at all familiar to the officers, the most senior amongst them reduced to jotting something down, if only as evidence he'd followed required procedure on arrival at the scene.

They'd departed with a warning to the four to stick to the local bye-laws and a promise they'd likely be back at some point, and a suggestion to avoid public places as far as was possible – still looking over their shoulder as they mounted the steps to return to their car. Traffic offences, the odd domestic, the occasional burglary were routine stuff. But a bunch of Apes taking an afternoon dip in the sea?

Seated behind the groyne, watching the blue uniformed officers depart, Ape Four turned to Ape One.

'What did they want dad?' he said.

'Not sure son,' Ape One replied in Ape-Talk, following the officers' departure with an ever-watchful eye.

It was, in fact, a sign of things to come.

With news of the new arrivals soon spreading – within days onlookers began assembling where the four were known to be residing, often in twos and threes – some peering from doorways or leaning over balconies in anticipation of one or more of the Apes putting in an appearance.

'They Apes?' their youngest would ask. They'd seen Apes at the zoo or on tele and seen pictures of them in books, but seeing them in the flesh was a quite different proposition.

Their parents would nod, exchanging looks with other adults whilst keeping quiet as to the potential implications.

The kids were intrigued, each eager to be the first to grab the Apes' attention.

'Oi Ape!' they'd shout when one of the younger occupants appeared from behind a shed or was seen peeping from behind a downstairs curtain. Nudging each other at the sight of a furry head appearing, and all too quickly disappearing from view.

In the streets and in supermarket queues the talk was of little else.

'What was it all about?'

'What are they doing here?'

'Why on earth would a family of Apes seek residency – permanent or otherwise – in a small coastal town in the UK?'

It was by popular demand that an emergency meeting was held at a packed town-hall. A chance for the more vocal members of the community to rise to their feet armed with a barrage of questions. The Conservative Leader Of The Council demanding to know how a family of Apes had secured residency in the borough, with – to the best of most people's knowledge – no advance warning and not a single contingency measure in place.

Midst the rancor and fingers levelled in all manner of directions, dissenting voices were to be heard – confirmation there'd been no reports of anti-social behaviour and that since their arrival the Apes had made a point of abiding by the laws and keeping a low profile.

That Ape-One continued to turn up dutifully at his place of work: a corner of the local park where he was paid the going rate for entertaining the locals by strutting around in a pair of jodhpurs pursing lips at cameras and posing for selfies with the kids. His wife, Ape-Two doing her bit at a local care-home where she prepared tea and biscuits for the residents before tucking them into her beds. Whilst the youngest – Apes-Three and Four – had settled into their schools with virtually no issues. Ape-Four, the very youngest – adored by the children who had warmed to him immediately, taking it in turns to cradle him in their arms rocking him back and forth and tweaking his toes in an attempt to make him feel at home.

But as is often the case with families of Apes seeking to settle in largely unfamiliar surroundings, there was more going on behind the scenes than first met the eye.

A second meeting, convened at the behest of Residents' Associations, prompting the Leader Of The Council's pronouncement that – this being the UK – the people's voices would be heard. That a forthcoming referendum would be held; ballot-boxes to be located at all registered voting stations where ballot-papers would require a cross against one of two options:

Apes should stay.....
Apes should go.....

Simplified later to...*Apes stay...Apes go*...so as to avoid confusion amongst some residents.

Within days the town had become a full-scale battleground: accusations flying via tabloid headlines, tv, radio – slogans splashed across the sides of buses.

'What's it all about dad?' Ape-Three would ask, peering through a gap in the curtains at babies wielded back and forth in prams bearing placards:

No Apes – No Dogs.....
Reclaim The Borders...

'Not sure son,' Ape-One replied, continuing to stare beyond the gate and urging his child to step back from the glass.

Which – though a diplomatic enough answer to a relatively innocent question – wasn't entirely true.

What *was* clear to Ape-One and his wife Ape-Two in their quieter moments – and to anyone who took time and trouble to observe the comings and goings in the world around them – was that a wind-of-change was in the air; that – as in the case of many a family of Apes seeking to settle in unfamiliar territory, particularly in the more isolated coastal communities – the writing was, in some cases, quite literally – on the wall.

It was some three to four days later that, shortly before midnight, a line of figures armed with bags was to be spotted taking a light night stroll along the promenade apparently intent on taking a late night dip in the sea.

A group that, on closer examination, proved not to be people, but a line of Apes, each carrying a back-pack and on descending the steps, making their way single-file to the water's edge where they came to a halt.

'Where are we heading dad?' Ape-Four had asked, keeping a firm grip on his father's hand.

'Not sure son...' came the reply. Ape-One's eye fixed for a while on some distant point of the ocean, before turning, urging the three to follow – each tip-toeing one by one in strict military formation.

Until, some five minutes later – Apes One to Four had disappeared from sight beneath a line of thin moonlit waves.

✳ ✳ ✳ ✳ ✳

The Man By The Gate

The two women walking the length of the clifftop stood a while, warming to the sight and sound of a gale-force wind bashing waves the size of mountains into rocks a hundred or so feet beneath them.

Moments to be cherished for those privileged to be living at such close quarters – each urging the other to grip more tightly so as not to lose their footing in the tufts of grass. And to take special care as they turned – arms linked, heads bowed to tackle the few hundred yards to their cottage in what were unquestionably perilous conditions.

The cottage was only a few hundred yards away, yet on a day such as this might have been a mile away; easy to miss unless you were actually looking for it. Hands reached to aid the other's progress and steady themselves against the elements, a hint of rain that could well be heading in a hail of bullets in their direction.

It was a few yards further that a hand tugged at the other's arm. And seconds later that the pair drew to a halt.

Someone was standing by their gate. On first glance, a man wearing a long coat and what, from a distance, appeared to be one of those old-fashioned trilby-type hats. The women exchanged looks but said nothing, each feeling for the other's hand, aware there was little alternative to continuing their short walk to the gate and that what transpired on their arrival remained to be seen and was largely out of their hands.

The man had hardly moved which suggested he might be waiting for them. Cause enough to stop and consider what his business might be.

He allowed them to get within earshot before seeing fit to speak – anticipating and thus prepared for the reception he might receive.

'Apologies for springing on you in such a fashion.' He spoke in a voice almost too soft to be audible in such conditions, looking over his shoulder as he did so. 'I happened to be passing and whilst pausing a while to admire your home I looked up and noticed two slates had come loose towards the lower end of your roof.'

He turned, directing both his and the women's attention to a side of the building that in the course of a day might easily get overlooked.

'On looking closer I saw the two slates sitting close to the gutter.' He had removed his hat, revealing black hair swept to near-collar length at the base of his neck.

'So I took it upon myself to replace the tiles.' He replaced his hat and looked in the direction of the two women stood hand-in-hand and appearing to be hanging onto his every word. 'I saw the ladder against the wall. Then I saw the shed and thought maybe there'd be something to ram the tiles into place, if you see what I mean...like a hammer.'

'That was kind,' said Maggie, the younger of the two sisters thinking it was time one of them spoke up.

'Very kind.' Alice had allowed the grip on her sister's arm to relax a little.

The man turned his attention to a sign swinging back and forth from an archway above their heads, his features temporarily hidden from view.

'I have to confess it was your sign that actually caught my attention.'

All three looked at the slate with *Bed & Breakfast* still clear enough to be read from the path.

The women relaxed, each leaning for support into the other's shoulder, Alice taking a moment to compose herself, Maggie quickly following suit.

'Now we understand,' she said.

It had taken a while for the penny to drop. The man stepped back, unsure as to the source of the amusement but happy to have apparently contributed to it.

Alice took a few steps and was looking to the highest point of the arch. 'It goes back a while.'

'It goes back to the last owners.'

The man listened whilst continuing to eye the sign and manoeuvre his hat between the fingers of one hand. 'Which is a long time ago now.'

'More than thirty years.'

'They were the last owners.'

All three looked again at the sign above the entrance. All was beginning to slot into place. The property had changed hands from past owners some time ago and the two women were the current owners.

'I didn't realise,' he said. The women shook their heads.

'Well...it's an easy mistake to make.'

'You're not listed then.'

The women looked at the man, and then at each other.

'Listed?'

'Listed. In a directory or an accommodation guide.'

There was stifled laughter.

'No...no.'

'Nothing like that.'

Again, the women composed themselves to speak.

'You see it doesn't happen.'

'Not anymore.'

'Not now.'

The man fidgeted, embarrassed to be jumping to such conclusions, and in conditions sufficient to try anyone's patience.

'Oh well....that's a shame.'

He looked up and then back along the stretch of path where the women had first been spotted. 'I was looking for somewhere, just for the night. And when I saw your cottage, and then saw the sign I thought...'

All three looked again at the source of the confusion. He'd spotted the sign and on seeing the two of them in the immediate vicinity and shortly after, making their way towards the gate – put two and two together and waited on their return. The truth was they hardly gave the sign a moment's thought given they rarely, if ever, had visitors.

What was equally clear, was that it was getting late and the likelihood of coming across a *Bed And Breakfast* at this hour and in a location such as this was virtually nil.

Alice was thinking that removing the sign after all these years might not be a bad idea. But time was getting on and unless they asked the man to take it down for them – which seemed a bit of an imposition given he'd already done them one huge favour. And with him needing to be getting along to find some accommodation for the night. The women exchanged looks. The weather was closing in and maybe a decision was called for.

'Well...we do have a room.'

'A spare room.'

'A very small room,' Maggie explained.

The man looked beyond the hedgerow marking the dividing line between public and private property: the women's bit of land he baulked to be seen intruding upon. The last thing he wanted was for them to be putting themselves out on his behalf.

'It doesn't seem right,' he said. 'Putting upon you in such a fashion.'

'Well...' Both had been thinking along similar lines: that whilst leaving the man to his own devices wouldn't be viewed as unreasonable, in that offering someone you didn't know – particularly a man – a room for the night, and at the drop of a hat, was not a decision to be taken lightly – he *had* done them a favour. And searching for a *Bed And Breakfast* at this hour – on such an afternoon as this – would be a thankless, not to say, hopeless task.

There was a wash-basin in the room and some spare bedding in the cupboard. Each appeared to be waiting for the other to make a decision. Being the eldest Alice thought maybe it was down to her to speak up.

'I have to say there'd be little chance of finding anywhere else...'

'Round these parts.'

'And at this time of day.'

'Well, that's very kind. Thankyou. Thankyou very much.'

On having the offer accepted, the women turned to their door. There'd be opportunity to consider the implications later. It was only for a night and it wasn't as if they didn't have the space. And rain – possibly torrential rain – seemed set to arrive at any moment.

Once inside the man stood a moment to take in the stroke of good fortune to have come his way, warming to the old-fashioned feel these seaside cottages seemed to exude.

A second door opened onto a living room complete with sofa and a pair of matching chairs. A bookcase stood close to an old-fashioned transistor-type radio.

'This is the main room,' Alice said.

'The downstairs bit,' said Maggie, aware the upstairs-bit would be their initial port-of-call.

Maggie was already heading for the kitchen. Behind her Alice was taking coats to a stand in the hallway.

'It's a fine place,' the man said, handing over his hat and relieved to be on the receiving end of such hospitality after an afternoon spent tramping the coast in near gale-force conditions.

Alice reached to hang the hat alongside the coat on the most convenient hook. Behind her Maggie was lighting a stove so they could get the kettle on.

'Tea!'

'Sounds wonderful.' The man stood, sweeping flaps of hair to the nape of his neck and looking to see which seat he'd be expected to occupy.

Alice was back from hanging the coats.

'So...the spare room. It's small, but hopefully it will suffice for a night.' Maggie had emerged from the kitchen wondering if she ought to be present when showing the man his room. Though there wasn't actually a great deal to show him: a bed, a cupboard, a table with just enough room to put a cup and saucer, a sink. Plus – there was no call to be crowding him in what wasn't a great deal of space. The honour of showing their guest to what was to be his room for the night would be left to her older sister. They hardly ever set foot in the room themselves, aside from occasional dusting and wiping of the windows.

The room appeared to meet his approval, Alice hovering at the door waiting for him to complete a brief inspection. After which, a moment left to himself might not be a bad idea. He had no luggage so it wasn't as if he'd be needing lots of cupboard space.

The man smoothed a corner of the bed and turned to face his host.

'It's fine, honestly. And by the way, my name's Davis, John Davis.' Extending a hand hardly seemed appropriate. Alice gave her name and that of her sister.

'No need to be too formal,' he said.

'Oh no, not at all.' Alice had remembered the spare bedding in the drawer. He thanked her, assuring her he'd deal with it shortly.

'Well...I'll leave you to it.'

She was thanked once again and seconds later was back to the living room where her sister was waiting. The pair coming face to face for the first time.

'What do you think?'

'He seems nice.' Alice was looking round, eager not to have her voice to carry beyond the foot of the stairs. 'We couldn't let him go looking for *Bed & Breakfast* on an afternoon like this.'

'Not along this stretch of coastline.'

'He'd never find anywhere.' Alice drew her sister to one side.

'Supposing...' Her voice had dropped, wanting to share a concern since first escorting him through the door. 'He offers us money.'

Maggie shook a head.

'We really shouldn't be taking his money.'

'No, I know. But supposing he insists?'

The possibility of him forcing money on them couldn't be discounted. Even though it couldn't have been further from their minds. It wasn't as if it was a *Bed & Breakfast* arrangement. They were simply doing him a favour.

They were in agreement just as Davis reappeared and crossed the floor to join them. Alice realised she'd forgotten to tell Maggie his name. She could tell her later. Or he could tell her himself. First, there was tea to deal with.

He'd finished viewing what proved to be an excellent room with an equally excellent view from the window, placing his few belongings on a bedside table before giving the mattress a quick squeeze and the taps on the sink in the corner a quick turn, finally wiping his mouth on a nearby towel.

'Mr. Davis.' Maggie crossed to meet him, her eye lowered to avoid direct contact.

'We were just saying.'

Davis had perched himself on the arm of a nearby chair.

'That you mustn't think of offering us payment.'

'For the room.'

'The point...*Our* point being...it isn't that sort of place.'

'A *Bed & Breakfast* place.'

'At least not anymore.'

Relieved to have cleared the air in that respect they stood back to hear what – if anything – he had to say on the subject.

'We'll see___'

'No!' Both were adamant, Alice instantly turning away, on this occasion happy to leave the talking to her sister.

Back in the kitchen, Maggie joined her only when the subject had been laid to rest. More immediate matters were pending, a pair of heads reappearing moments later from behind the door.

'If you'd like to eat with us....'

'It would be no problem.'

They'd discussed the issue in private, agreeing it would only be fair to offer the man something to eat or what on earth was he going to do for food?

'Well that's very kind.' Davis stood awkwardly, sticking to his habit of seeking to keep the extent of his gratitude in check.

'Not a bit of it.'

'It's no trouble.'

'No trouble at all.'

Maggie looked over her shoulder, the women's reasoning – that it was as easy to put a loaf of bread on the table for two as for one, and therefore for three as for two – was straightforward enough.

'You're very kind,' he said.

'Not at all.'

Alice was back from the kitchen, a tray clutched in one hand.

'Biscuits?'

All three took their seats, and with the arrangements sorted with minimum fuss and what remained of the day ahead of them – responsibility for striking up conversation would be down to the two sisters. Though opportunities for conversing with anyone other than each other had, for some years, been rare, not to say non-existent – especially with a man. Albeit a man of few words which both knew was often the case with men. As was frequently the case with *them* given they could hardly be described as social creatures.

Davis got to hear how they'd come by the property close to thirty years ago, formerly living in town but becoming disenchanted with the hustle and bustle and what they considered to be the ignorance of some townsfolk.

The women watched Davis pursue his habit of periodically getting to his feet to take in the view from the window.

'He seems very fond of the place,' Alice had observed later whilst helping out in the kitchen, the pair agreeing to leave the man to his own devices for a while.

'It's lucky we were around when he happened to be passing.'

'Lucky for him,' Maggie said.

'And he hasn't said anything more about money,' Alice remarked.

'I don't think we'll hear anything more on that score. I think we made it perfectly clear where we stood on the issue.'

'I wonder...' Alice took three mugs and turned to a jug of milk. 'What time he retires for the night.'

'Probably not too early I would imagine – men that age.' Both had been wondering how the evening was set to pan out once the table had been cleared. 'I suppose we could retire earlier than him. I don't see any reason why not.'

'Not at all. I mean – I think we can trust him.' Maggie stopped to peer over her sister's shoulder. 'I mean...there's nothing of value kept down here.'

'No, absolutely not.' Alice stopped to consider the implications of her sister's remark. 'Maybe it's a bit bad of us to be thinking along such lines. I mean he seems a decent enough chap.'

'Well I wasn't thinking there was a risk as such. It's just... you know___'

Each understood the other's point: that they were justified in being on their guard. When you lived alone at their age and rarely had visitors you couldn't be too careful about these things.

Maggie had continued peering through the gap in the door to see what, if any developments were afoot.

'What's he about?'

'Nothing much. Just looking. Staring into space.'

'One of his habits.' Alice moved closer to the door.

'Clearly a creature of habit.'

'Of many habits.'

There was a chuckle as Alice turned to pans hanging from a line of hooks.

'What weather!' With little more to occupy them it was back to the conversation from earlier.

'Terrible,' Alice observed from her corner of the sofa.

'Set to remain for a few days,' Davis remarked, placing his cup on the table and looking round. 'Or at least tomorrow.' The weather reports were full of it. And not just in this county.'

'It's often the same in these parts.'

'When it rains, it pours.'

There were more chuckles from the seat behind. Maggie made a move to replenish the biscuit tray. Davis broke a length of shortbread on his plate and turned to speak.

'So – you've been here some time.' Though wary of seeming intrusive he was interested to hear the circumstances that had brought the women to such an idyllic – if isolated spot.

'Oh a long time...'

'Years.' Maggie was back from the kitchen, placing a tray midway between the sofa and the chairs. A quick calculation followed. 'Thirty two years.'

'Yes – thirty-two in March.'

Davis was impressed. It was quite a stint in one place, even a place like this. He'd hardly stayed six months in some of the places he'd lived.

'You must like it here.' The irony – if intended – failed to make an impression.

'Oh...we love it.'

'What we *really* like is the peace and quiet.'

'And the sea.'

'And the wind sometimes.'

'And sometimes even the rain.'

'That was what struck us when we first viewed the place.'

'Was that through an agent?' Davis reached for the biscuit tray, keen to hear more though still wary of delving into matters that might be viewed as none of his business. You didn't often get to hear how properties in such locations as this exchanged hands.

'I think so yes.'

'But he's gone now.'

'Went abroad I think.'

'Years ago.'

Recollections of the time were increasingly hazy. But it was interesting to be reminded of old ground if not to the last detail. And to his credit Davis was proving to be a good listener.

'So – having no ties must be a real plus.'

'Ties?'

'Ties...' Davis half-turned to face them. 'Responsibilities. Nothing doing with estate-agents and the like.'

'Oh no...It's so long ago we don't have any responsibilities of that kind...agents and people such as that.'

'No mortgage then.' Davis took a second biscuit, temporarily held aloft as if for brief examination.

'Mortgage?'

'You know...money owed on the property. To the bank or building society. The perils of home-ownership.' He continued to stare at the biscuit extended in the fingers of one hand. 'No dealings with financiers or solicitors and the like.'

'Oh no...'

'Nothing like that.'

'As our father would have put it...'

'Neither a borrower nor a lender be,' said Maggie.

'That was always our father's motto.'

'And ours too.'

'One of the perks of living as we do.'

'The way we like it.'

Davis settled in his seat, eyes raised to the ceiling in quiet acknowledgement of a lifestyle with evidently much to commend it.

'And not a million miles from my own disposition to these things, let me tell you that. So – what about friends and family?'

The women were quiet for a moment, Alice eventually speaking on behalf of them both.

'We don't have friends.

'And the family have all gone,' Maggie added, speaking without any obvious tone of regret.

'As in – passed on,' Alice explained.

For a moment the room fell silent.

'I'm afraid we're very much loan wolves,' Maggie said finally. 'But we *do* like it that way.'

Davis saw off what remained of his coffee and leant back in his chair.

'And – where's the harm in that?' he said, speaking with some emphasis and with a slap of a hand on each arm of the chair. 'We are what we are, and no-one, but *no-one* can ever take that from us.'

With their tale more or less told, the women were curious as to *his* circumstances. How a man his age – walking alone – came to be stalking the coastline in such weather and with little apparent thought as to his evening's accommodation.

But it would have to wait. There was a stirring in the chair – an idea that had been brewing since first taking up the offer of a bed for the night.

'I've been thinking...'

The women exchanged looks. Some suggestion about to be put to them – hopefully having nothing to do with money passing hands.

'Tomorrow...' Davis was back to another habit of tracing a finger on the chair arm when at the point of speaking. 'Why don't I look around and see if there are any jobs to be done? Quick jobs? Tidying up your shed perhaps. There's stuff in there going back years I should imagine.'

The women looked to each other for a reaction. Certainly, it was an offer not to be instantly dismissed. The shed would likely be in a bit of a state after all these years, not having set foot in it for as long as they could remember. On conferring, agreement was reached – but with some qualification.

'Well that's very kind of you Mr. Davis.'

'But___'

'Only a bit. We don't want you putting yourself out on our behalf.'

A qualification swiftly brushed aside. The hospitality on offer more than enough to redress the balance.

It was the moment for Alice to be reminded of a bottle of dry sherry they'd had sitting in a cupboard since a previous Christmas.

'Will you take a drop of sherry Mr. Davis?' She was already out of her chair and heading for a tray of glasses.

'I don't mind if I do. Thank you. Thank you very much.'

The opening of a cabinet door was followed by a clink of glass and popping of a cork. A glass later handed to Davis, accepted with a further token of gratitude.

'You're too kind.'

'Not at all.'

'Here's to you both,' said Davis, raising the glass. 'But...'

He drank slowly before reaching to place the glass on a nearby table. 'Back to tomorrow. Before we get round to clearing garden sheds, I was thinking a brisk early morning walk might be in order. Maybe a stroll along the cliff path. You ladies know the lie of the land and I imagine it's quite something to witness the elements at close hand in such conditions as we're currently experiencing.'

He continued to stare into the glass's contents whilst slowly rotating the stem between finger and thumb.

What might have had half the women's attention on the seat behind suddenly had Alice's entire concentration. The answer – when it finally arrived – delivered in a voice Davis would struggle to hear.

'A sight to behold indeed. Which was the case when you first spotted us, if you recall the moment Mr. Davis.'

Maggie knew from experience there were occasions when it paid to let her sister do the talking. Both their eyes were on Davis, leaning back effortlessly in his chair, and at the point of raising his glass.

'Good health ladies.'

'Likewise Mr. Davis.'

'Good health indeed...' said Alice.

Without a further word spoken Davis nodded approval as the three continued to make light work of the bottle's contents – the evening from here-on in allowed to drift in whatever direction it chose.

A brisk wind met a closing of the door as the three made their way toward the sign still swinging freely in the space above their heads.

A day for sou'westers and scarves with conversation of any description off the agenda for the time being.

First stop was a spot by a bend in the path running alongside the edge of the cliff, a path the pair had followed yesterday where Alice had realised – on examining her coat pocket at the conclusion of the evening – she'd possibly dropped a ring of beads whilst taking a handkerchief from her pocket. A memento from years past she'd taken to keeping permanently in her possession. A minor detour but, if only for sentimental reasons, worth a quick look.

A wilder day would be difficult to picture. The women clutching each other's arms as they eased their way to the spot where Alice was fairly sure she must have dropped the beads, remembering them being in her pocket when they'd stopped to view the scene below. Davis agreeing to act as a wind-break for the minute or so it would take her to get down on hands and knees to forage in the few feet close to the edge of the cliff.

A more painstaking operation than they'd imagined, Maggie's warnings to her sister prompting Davis to keep a closer eye on proceedings with an offer of further assistance if required.

There was a good bit of shuffling in the grass until she paused and leant closer.

'Aha!' The exclamation drew both their attention, Davis largely unaware of Maggie shifting into position behind him.

Whether a gesture of celebration or simply her way of breaking the silence – he would never know.

On uttering the exclamation – Alice had gripped tufts of grass with whatever strength her ageing arms could muster, arching herself into the wet grass, just as Maggie – glancing repeatedly left and right – launched herself into Davis, sending him toppling over Alice's kneeling body and seconds later – with an exclamation of his own neither could quite catch – stumbling and then tumbling and finally plummeting over the cliff, eventually coming to rest flopped across an arc of rocks a hundred or so feet beneath them.

Instantly the women were back on their feet, Maggie's attempt to peer into the abyss for confirmation of Davis's demise, swiftly aborted by her sister – each gripping the other as they stepped back from the edge and found the path to return them quickly to their cottage.

Neither had known, or even suspected, they had it in them – slamming the door behind them and instantly shaking the worst of the wind and rain from hats and collars, turning to the panes of glass where a scene of desolation hung in the wind and rain stretching the whole length of the coastline.

'That was close.'

'*Extremely* close.' Both were fighting for breath, Alice struggling to regain her composure whilst needing to know her sister's thinking was still in line with her own.

'You *do* see...we had no choice.' She was leaning to find the energy to speak, the events of the last few minutes sufficient to leave her breathless for the change of surroundings to take effect. 'You do see that?'

Maggie's eye had barely moved from the *Bed & Breakfast* sign for once swinging almost sedately beneath the arch of the gate.

'His mistake was suggesting a walk. I mean...why would anyone choose to go walking along the cliffs in such conditions as this...?'

A hand found its way onto her sister's arm, urging her to leave events beyond the window to their own devices for a moment.

'Unless he was up to something,' Maggie said, repeating her sister's line from earlier that morning.

Both were back to the window, each seeking assurance their suppositions were sound: that when a man arrives out of the blue with no luggage, accepts an offer of accommodation for the night and then sets about seeking information as to their past, discovers they have no friends, no family – no contact with solicitors, estate-agents...there has to be a reason.

'And....' Alice turned to face her sister. 'What he needed to realise was...we'd never have been safe. If it hadn't been today it could have been tomorrow. Or the day after.'

'Or the day after that.'

'Or *any* day.'

'Or any week...'

'Or month!'

'For as long as we both shall live!'

Maggie watched Alice head for a chest of drawers where she began rummaging idly through its contents.

'It just seems odd that he didn't appear to appreciate any of that,' Maggie said quietly, turning to where the rain continued an unrelenting pelting of the glass.

She looked back over her shoulder.

'Do you think there were any tiles missing?'

'Tiles?'

'On the roof. The tiles that he claimed to have put back in place.'

Alice thought for a moment before turning to a second stack of clothing in the drawer.

'Who knows? Probably not I'd say.'

'I suppose that's one question we'll never know the answer to,' Maggie said, back to the window as her sister closed the drawer and turned to cross the few feet of space that divided them.

'What *is* certain – is that in these conditions anyone getting too close can lose their footing and go toppling over the cliff.'

'Not to mention suicides.'

'Suicides...accidents. In these conditions – absolutely anything's possible.'

Maggie turned from the window attempting to force a smile but somehow not quite managing it.

* * * * *

The Queen's Visit

The brown foolscap envelope landing in the hallway of Mr. and Mrs. Barnoldswick's home one April morning was to have considerable repercussions. It was Barnoldswick's wife who leaned to pick the envelope from the mat and seeing her husband's name typed on the front, took it to the breakfast room where her husband sipped tea between taking bites of toast.

'For you dear.'

Putting his toast to one side, he took the envelope and tore its flap, taking the A4 size sheet and casting an eye over its contents.

'My God...' he said. 'Good gracious.'

His wife looked up. Clearly a matter of some import to prompt such a reaction, her husband rarely one for such outbursts of emotion. Her husband finished reading the letter, then read it a second time, then a third – *one* to take in the impact of what he was reading, but also to check he'd got the details absolutely right.

The source of the exclamation was, for sure, the kind of thing that would stop anyone in their tracks to check they weren't in the midst of some weird dream. But there it was in black and white: In little more than a few months' time, The Queen, as in...Her Majesty The Queen Of England...would be visiting their tiny Hertfordshire village. The communication, with its official-looking lettering and equally official-looking insignia grafted onto the top corner of the page – currently in the hands of Barnoldswick's wife — confirming that the event was scheduled to occur on a Thursday afternoon of the 24th July at approximately fifteen minutes past three.

Barnoldswick did a quick bit of maths. Three months slightly more.

The explanation – if one were needed – that the Royal Party would be journeying by car following an appointment in The Midlands; a personal request of Her Majesty to take advantage of travelling by car to familiarise herself with a side of life too often overlooked in these more global times. Not that she'd be staying long. More…passing through it on a re-routed journey on account of engineering work on one of the local highways.

Barnoldswick settled on his elbows to award himself a bit of thinking time.

After which he took the letter to his study to seat himself in his hand-me-down chair from his great-grandfather to award serious thought to what would unquestionably be the most momentous event in the history of the village of Upper Twaddle, the preparations for which – Barnoldswick had already made clear in his own mind – would leave absolutely nothing to chance.

In respect of which, this was to be not so much *his* day as *everyone's* day: the village, the community – in fact the whole county would have its part to play with the eyes of the nation upon it, and with everyone taking their share of the credit. Which – by implication [if you wished to view it that way] – was set to make G. Barnoldswick a key figure not just in terms of local history but in the entire history of rural England…

Quite a thought seated at his humble desk in his no less humble abode of 9 St. Cheviot's Close (first right after the Coop) in the village of Upper Twaddle, Hertfordshire.

He immediately reached for a sheet of A4 paper, flattening it to set about logging a provisional *List Of Responsibilities And Designated Posts*. But first – phone-calls to a few eminent persons: the vicar, Mrs. Bowles who did the accounts for the Summer-fetes and Christmas raffles and the local constabulary, who – on checking their in-tray – could confirm they'd received similar intelligence late the previous afternoon.

The responsibilities would – out of necessity if nothing else – be a team-effort. But as an honorary Leader Of The Council – G. Barnoldswick would be very much in the driving seat when it came to overseeing arrangements and duties, his first task being to chair a meeting to establish what the visit would entail and to consider all implications.

The meeting, held two days later in the village hall, agreed on four key designated areas: *Guide And Escort Duties... Catering...Decorations...Formal Greetings & Introductions...*

It also ran through a likely course of events, the finer details of which would – courtesy of the communication – be left to the hosts beyond establishing that the car would draw to a halt in the centre of the village allowing opportunity for Her Majesty to stretch her legs, get a quick flavour of the place and return to the car to resume her journey to London.

What *stretching her legs* and getting a *flavour of the place* would actually entail would be down to those who knew the area and would be in position to arrange a suitable itinerary. A provisional sketch on the white-board at the front of the hall suggesting that if she exited the car by a left hand door, stood by the door to accept the greetings of the welcoming party, she'd walk at a leisurely pace along the road probably in a northerly direction for something like one to two hundred yards before returning to the car to deliver a parting wave to the crowds lining the opposite side of the road.

Which meant appointing a foreman (or foreperson) proposed and seconded for each area of responsibility starting from where the car would stop and Her Majesty would alight.

It was the following morning that a team of four gathered round the spot where the royal car would come to a halt. The assumption being that since they were arriving from the midlands they'd be facing south, which meant stepping onto a grass verge on the left hand side between two lamp-posts. Though still largely grass, it was seen to be thinning in places and could, in inclement weather, get a little muddy and slippery underfoot. A proposal to have the area cleared of weeds and a four metre stretch of turf laid between the two lamp posts was instantly approved.

Following Her Majesty's exit from the car the path was in generally good condition. A few leaves could be swept away at one point and a rather overgrown hedge would need trimming back. Mrs. Oswaldtwistle, the owner of the property had her son over most weekends and he could likely be trusted to address the problem during the interim period.

On return to her car, a half dozen schoolchildren would be on hand armed with a bouquet of flowers to greet Her Majesty along with a tray of Mrs. Moggin's all-butter muffins presented by the great-granddaughter of Mrs. Walker-Myles-Gibson, one of the village's oldest residents whose husband had supposedly seen action on a number of fronts in two world wars. The children would be fitted in red, blue and white: white tops, blue skirts or in the case of the boys, trousers and red socks, blue ties. The possibility of including a black – or *coloured* child as the more elderly members of the community were apt to describe them – was raised, a touch that might go down well in Royal circles with so many countries in the Empire (as was) still clinging to memories of a past era. The only problem – confirmed on further investigation – that the nearest black child was in the town seventeen miles away and would need to be bussed in for the day. A not insurmountable problem but one that, along with one or two other issues, could be put on the back-burner for now. Another being concern at Her Majesty coming face to face with *A Spotted Cock* – the name of the local pub the Royal entourage would pass about fifty yards into their walkabout. A suggestion to change C to R for the day probably the most practical solution.

On returning to the car Her Majesty would watch the children perform a dance round the maypole after being presented with a second bouquet of flowers by a little girl called Agnes – great-grandchild of Mrs. Mason-Baines the eldest resident who'd lived in the village for eighty six years before passing away late Christmas Eve the previous year.

As to the dignitaries on-hand to greet The Party, it was agreed Barnoldswick, (adopted leader-of-the-council) Mrs. Appledore – daughter of a viscount having served on two battle fronts but sadly passing away the previous year, the vicar and the Head Of The Highways committee who'd received public commendation for helping the village acquire a listing in the latest edition of *AA Guide To Rural England* should be awarded pride of place..

A final touch but hardly one to be overlooked – fifty boxes of union-jack flags to be provided by a shop in town. Each child would be issued with one, plus members of the crowd closest to the car. Advice being to hold the flag at head height or slightly higher and wave it manically as the car arrived and drew to a halt. Accompanied by a cheer as Her Majesty exited the car and turned to face the crowd. And then later as she returned from her walkabout and prepared to make her departure. The number of flags required would be difficult to gauge; enough to decorate every rooftop in the vicinity plus the butchers, the bakers, Mrs. Edwards' florist shop, the mini-Coop next door and the entrance to the church though questions were raised in some quarters as to how God might feel about having His property adorned in flags; general consensus being He might not object as long as it was restricted to the arch over the entrance.

One thing that was difficult to plan for was the weather, a contingency plan needed were Her Majesty to be stepping onto wet grass, freshly laid or not. Fortunately it turned out not to be an issue – the weather forecast closer to the day predicting clear skies with a light scattering of cloud.

It was at a meeting forty-eight hours prior to the visit that points listed on four sides of A4 were read aloud and ticked to ensure it was all systems go and that all eventualities had been covered. A meeting ending with a shaking of hands and a glass of beer or sherry in *The Spotted Rock*.

All that remained was to sit it out and wait.

For once the weathermen were spot on with their predictions: a thin cloud allowing a thin sun to creep onto the scene during late afternoon. Before which it was quite a performance in the households and shops of Upper Twaddle: Mrs. Moggin beavering away over an oven full of muffins, Mrs. Edwards checking her boxes of roses were signed sealed and ready for delivery to their appointed spot, Jack – the part-time fireman standing on his ladder – draping the last few yards of flags over garage doors partly in view of where the Royal Party would alight.

It was with watches checked at just before midway through the afternoon, that the dignitaries made their way – suits pressed, shoes polished, in the case of Mrs. Barnoldswick a new skirt in red and blue chiffon, puffed out at the seams – to the centre of the village where they greeted the already assembled crowd and surveyed chains of flags attached to roofs of shops, and did another quick check on the re-tufted area where Her Majesty would exit the car, ensuring each bit had settled firmly into place. After which it was all eyes on the displays and beyond, where the schoolchildren's dance-group was on hand to play their part as and when called upon to do so.

It was at round three pm. that they got themselves into a line between the two lamp-posts where Mrs. Agnes's grandchild stood armed with Mrs. Moggins' all-butter muffins and a tray of specially prepared fairy-cakes topped in red white and blue icing.

Another look at watches. The children – flags at the ready as per instruction – were looking eagerly to their left, keen to be the first to spot a big black car purring into sight a few hundred yards up the road.

More glances at watches. The vicar approached Barnoldswick who, in turn, approached one of the four constables on duty their side of the road, just to check each other's take on the time.

They were some way behind schedule: a strain of frustration beginning to show amongst some sections of the crowd, many of whom – being well into their senior years and in some cases non-too-steady on their feet – had been standing for close to two hours, waving their flags and cheering merrily at reporters seeking to capture the moment on camera for a special edition of the local paper the following week. The children too were becoming a little restless, having stood around for something close to an hour with little sign of anything happening.

Another check with watches. Huddled conversations now on both sides of the road – all assuming the engineering work must be the source of what was soon to be an hour and fifteen minute delay. Despite numerous phone-calls there'd been no confirmation from the police nor any communication from official sources as to the cause of the delay.

All of which – in its way – was unfortunate. For had they taken the trouble to pack themselves off – Barnoldswick in his pressed suit, his wife in matching chiffon, Mrs. Moggins and her tray of fairy-cakes and crowds lining the road with their Union-Jack flags – and got themselves to a spot some fifty miles to the east and looked to the skies, they might just have caught the wing tips of a plane some thirty to thirty-five thousand feet above them. Aboard which...Her Majesty, an entourage of secretaries, two Secretaries Of State, Ambassadorial staff and a handful of Cabinet Ministers... would shortly be over French air-space en-route to a hastily convened G8 Heads-Of-State summit in Dubai.

Clearly, there'd be little point in them hanging around too long. For before anyone had a chance to thrust a homemade muffin aloft – or wave a Union Jack flag in their direction – they'd be over the sea and far away.

It was a week or two later that a brown foolscap envelope landed in the hallway of Mr. and Mrs. Barnoldswick's home. It was Barnoldswick's wife who leaned to pick the envelope from the mat and seeing her husband's name typed on the front, took it to the breakfast room where her husband sipped tea between taking bites of toast.

'For you dear.'

Putting his toast to one side, he took the envelope and tore its flap, taking the A4 size sheet and casting an eye over its contents.

Putting envelope and its contents to one side, he was quickly back to his tea and toast.

* * * * *

Margarita Time

[A sequel to…'Margarita' *Call These Stories,* 'Margarita-Mark-Two' *Telling Tales,* 'When Margarita Met Candice' *Stories For Airports.*]

Things aren't going too badly. I've recently moved into a new place – first floor, second on the right. I had to leave the old place because of one or two problems to do with the people there, some of whom were a bit odd. But if there's one thing I've learnt it's that if you took all the people in the world who are a bit odd and put them in one place you'd likely need somewhere the size of the British Isles to put them all. Basically there'd been complaints. The landlord, or whoever owned the property – I've never been sure how things like owners and landlords work when it comes to day-to-day running of flats – said there'd been complaints. I don't know why there had been complaints but apparently they were from people living close by, which is all he would say on the subject. I think it might have been the couple next door. When I used to pass them in the corridor from time to time when me and Margarita were off on one of our afternoon strolls or arriving back, they'd scowl and look fiercely into each other's eye. They were quite elderly which might have been part of the problem. It seems to me older people are sometimes quick to find things to take exception to. I think they might be religious too, which doesn't help. I once had a problem with a religious person who caught me and Margarita kissing in a deserted park and said living with Margarita was a sinful act, or me being with her was sinful. I can't remember which. As it doesn't hurt anyone and doesn't affect anyone else I can't see why it's sinful. I think telling people Jesus was born at Christmas is sinful because we don't know when he was born. Which means vicars are effectively telling lies, which is supposed to be a sin. Which just goes to show that when it comes to being a bit odd, religious people are often at the front of the queue.

Anyway I think they were the people who might have complained. Or maybe it was whoever lives beneath. I know the flats were a bit cramped and our bedroom was directly above the flat below's bedroom, and the Margaritas do tend to make the bed squeak when it rocks back and forth during our lovemaking. So maybe it was keeping them awake. When a note was popped through my door I went down to speak to her about it but she wouldn't open the door. She just said 'go away'. She wore glasses and was a bit on the big side. I know I shouldn't really say such things, but it made me wonder if there was a bit of jealousy. Margarita's slim with big eyes and a broad smile and wide pouting lips. I know some women tend to notice such things about other women and maybe it made her think about herself.

Anyway, I had to leave but I don't mind because the place I'm in now is better. The people where I live are a bit younger, some in their twenties or thirties and not one of them has said anything about Margarita. Some even say 'hi' when we pass on the stairs or coming in or out of the entrance which is a friendly side you don't always get in these kinds of properties or in people in general. Margarita appreciates it. I know this because her smile's always broader when we get back after passing a few words on the stairs. The soundproofing's better in these flats too. It means even when we're going at it *hammer and tongue* – as one of the men at the sex-class I once went to, used to put it when we shared our experiences with our partners – there's less chance of keeping people awake or having them hear us because I don't mind admitting I can get a bit carried away, especially with Margarita 'on top' coming out with some of her special vocabulary. She also likes to be in control in certain situations which can be pretty demanding but I don't mind because I like it when she takes the initiative, which I don't think is a bad thing and actually helps make our relationship stronger. I think if more men let women 'take the initiative' they'd maybe avoid a lot of problems.

Anyway we were quite settled in our new flat. You can look over the park which has a lake with ducks and tennis-courts at one end where we sometimes went for an afternoon stroll or to buy some things from the shops. Admittedly we did get some funny looks. I suppose people aren't accustomed to meeting women like Margarita, people with a smile for every occasion.

Though I have to explain that the current Margarita isn't my first partner, not by some way now. There were four before her – all with a rather unfortunate tale to tell. I lost the first when I accidentally burnt a hole in her leg with a cigarette after we'd made love for the first time. She just withered and died next to me on the sofa. But I learnt my lesson – that you need to watch what you're doing with your cigarette when relaxing after making love.[1]

It took a while to get over it but they say time's a great healer, and after a month or so I was off to the shop in Soho in town where I have got to know two of the women who work there and can advise you on things when you're choosing a new partner.

Margarita-Two was similar in many ways except her mouth was a bit wider – which is the way the modern-day Margaritas tend to be.

Things were going fine until an unfortunate incident in a pub where we'd arranged to meet a couple. I'd actually met the man in the same pub a few days beforehand and his partner called Candice who was near-enough identical to Margarita, bought at a shop very close to the one I went to. We were just having a quiet drink and the women were getting on fine. But there were some men in the pub who were looking in our direction and laughing as if something was funny. Disaster struck when one came over and tried to put a badge on Margarita which she hadn't asked for and didn't want. I tried to stop him but the man was laughing as he did it. I think he might have been a bit drunk. Him and his mates had been drinking for quite some time. As soon as he did it there was a bit of a struggle and I shouted for him to stop but he pushed me away and didn't stop. He just stuck the pin in Margarita who folded onto the bar and died in my arms like the first Margarita only this time in public. The man laughed and couldn't see I was annoyed and quite sad. In any case I can't see what was so funny. How would he like it if someone pricked him with a pin and he leant over the bar and died?[2]

Like the previous time, it took a while to get over it but you can't let the grass grow under your feet and before long I was off back to the shop in town where I was almost on first name terms with the women who work there.

'Back again,' they said as I entered the shop for the third time. Maybe they thought I was collecting Margaritas or running some sort of Margarita talent-contest. I gave a kind of explanation but didn't say much. There are some things you prefer to keep to yourself. They'd been equally sympathetic when I went to buy Margarita-Two but I wasn't going to say much about that. I wasn't going to tell them about burning a hole in Margarita' leg with a cigarette or they might have thought I'd done it on purpose and had me down as one of those men who gets his kicks out of hurting women. Or that I was just a bit stupid – which isn't as bad but still best avoided.

But the women said 'hi' and seemed pleased to see me. I think they're from Russia but it's difficult to be sure about people from that part of the world and I don't really like to ask. One of them looks a bit like Margarita though she's a bit broader in the hips and her breasts are bigger. Breasts are interesting. I know a lot of men think about breasts a lot, and talk about them, sometimes in a joking way. That happened a lot at the class. A lot of men like big breasts. Or *say* they like big breasts. It could be they were just saying that to be like other men. I'm not too bothered about them either way, but am probably biased because all Margaritas had or have quite small breasts; small but firm and jutting out like plastic cupcakes with a teat-bit on the end that I like to flick with my finger, or sometimes my tongue though I need to be careful not to get my teeth near them. I suppose in my own way I'm becoming something of a 'breast man' though not like some men who seem to talk of little else when it comes to women.

Anyway the women in the shop were happy to talk about breasts, and other things. They showed me one or two other models with names like *Naughty Naomi* and *Kiss-Me-Quick Cassandra*, sitting there on the top shelf, all with that wide-eyed look, waiting for the right man to come along. There were some differences which makes it worthwhile choosing, but what they all have in common is being slender, some with slightly wider eyes which give the impression they're really pleased to see you and that things are bound to be all right between you if you went ahead and chose her. Interestingly the mouths too tend to vary a lot though most of them are pretty large and usually wide open like they're about to say something or break into song, letting you know they'd be happy to join you given the opportunity. I think the idea is that they're kind of talking though not much. That they're more the quiet type which some men might prefer. The lady took two or three from the shelf for me to have a closer look, pointing out the different features and that some of them now have interchangeable hair styles, from shoulder-length blonde hair to close-cut dark hair. They asked me if I wanted a blonde or a brunette, or maybe a red-head. I went for the brunette as blonde is a bit showy and red-heads are sometimes said to be a bit on the fiery side. Apparently some have interchangeable heads which is an interesting idea but maybe taking things a bit far and in a way seems to defeat the point. If you want a partner with a different head, why choose her in the first place? What both women said was how much they'd changed since the early days when they were little more than rigid inflatables with stick-like legs and arms along the lines of a child's doll but with a wide open mouth. Nothing like a woman at all – whereas the modern ones tend to be authentic-looking in just about every respect.

Anyway, Margarita-Three looked fine – similar to *one* and *two* but a little shorter and with narrower shoulders. Once the business in the shop was sorted, the woman put her in a plastic bag until I got home. Getting her out on The Tube on the journey home to have a quick look and check the leaflet they give you, wasn't really practical as there isn't much room on the Tube.

But we got back and got settled and were getting on fine. Particularly in the physical sense, a side of the relationship that has always been a huge plus. I read somewhere that it's a big reason – in some cases the main reason – for so many relationships failing. Nearly one in three they say. Which is a shame, and in some ways stupid. I learnt quite a lot about this side of things in the class I went to: that couples can get bored with each other physically and look for a bit of excitement elsewhere. Or that it's to do with 'preferences' – what one of them likes to do but the other person doesn't. The thing about Margarita is you can quickly come to an arrangement where each is happy to do what the other wants, which means there are always new areas to explore; like Margarita telling me she likes to go on top but facing the other way so she can shout things without me hearing. Which is fine by me because you need to work at these things together. One thing all Margaritas have in common is none of them say much, but during sex they can come out with things that would make your hair curl. I mentioned it to the women in the shop and they laughed; something they're no doubt aware of but prefer not to talk about.

The class I went to advertises itself by claiming to 'broaden our horizons' which means thinking about what we get up to in bed. The woman who ran it – I think her name was Mave – would have each of us recount an experience which would then be discussed. And she would offer advice, looking at it from a woman's perspective. At first some of us were a bit shy and embarrassed to be talking about these things, like men are apt to be. But Mave was good at having you drop your inhibitions and speak freely, pointing out that sex is, or should be, a natural and beautiful experience. Which was when one of the men told us about giving his partner a 'damned good spanking'. Not because she'd done anything wrong, but as a bit of variety in bed. Mave said 'fine' as long as it's a two-way thing. I wasn't sure about giving Margarita a good spanking. It seems a bit cruel and she hadn't done anything to deserve being spanked, which I know isn't really the point but it's the way I look at it. Plus – it could have ended up with her bottom splitting and her going down on me.

But you get some good ideas from Mave and I bought a book she'd written: *Adding Spice To Your Sex Life* which is full of good advice and illustrations. A few of her suggestions wouldn't work with Margarita; the ones about 'sharing your fantasies' would be tricky as Margarita doesn't have a lot to say in the routine course of things.

But it isn't just about sex. They say a relationship founded solely on sex is likely to fail. We also liked to walk and watch tv. And sometimes go to the cinema, though that doesn't always work. Last time I was allowed in but Margarita wasn't. She had to stay in the cloakroom amongst the umbrellas and holdalls till the film was over. They gave me a ticket to make sure she didn't get lost or given to the wrong person. The man was laughing as he gave me the ticket but I didn't really enjoy the film. It's not the same watching it on your own, especially with your partner hanging around in the cloakroom waiting for the film to finish.

We sometimes read and Margarita liked me to read to her. We were working our way through *Shades Of Grey* but it's a bit hard-going in places. We tend to avoid pubs and discos. I've had some bad experiences in pubs I don't want to be repeated, and I'm a bit old for discos. What we sometimes do is put a CD on, maybe Frank Sinatra or Tony Bennet. I'll open a bottle of wine and turn the lights low and we'll dance the night away in my living room, which is a nice thing to do – a way of sharing your feelings for each other without going overboard about it or being on public view.

One of the good things about being with Margarita is she never looks any older. So as I get older, it's like having a relationship with a younger woman, which I quite like the idea of – that however old I get, and look, Margarita is still happy to be with me and I won't be with someone who is getting old and wrinkly. Not that there's anything wrong in looking old, or *being* old. I will be one day. Though when I see older people I can't help thinking they *want* to look that way. That as we get older we choose to have a hanging face and grey hair and wrinkles and walk with a stoop. Which I know is silly. You don't choose anything about growing old in terms of the way you look. But I have to say the idea of making love to someone old and wrinkled doesn't really appeal to me, which isn't being unkind because I know it can work both ways. I can't imagine women will find me attractive when I'm old and wrinkled. Except for Margarita, to whom things like that simply don't matter.

Anyway, I'm talking about Margarita Mark Three as if all is going well, and in most respects it was...

Until one afternoon with the Spring weather already upon us when I decided to do something different: a little surprise for Margarita as it was close to our anniversary. I went to book a ride on one of the boats on the River Thames. Something I'd never done and I thought it would be a treat for her – give her chance to sit back and feel the wind in her face for a few hours.

The men who ran the boat seemed a bit nonplussed when we climbed the steps to take our seats at the rear of the boat. Some smaller children were pointing and asking their mothers about Margarita, but they were quickly pulled away and taken to a different part of the boat. Which was fine by me as we had the whole rear of the boat to ourselves. All was going well and I was pointing out some of the sights to Margarita and was at the point of asking the man about a building we'd just passed – when a gust of wind blew over the side of the boat and in the split second I'd released Margarita's hand she did a backward somersault and was swept overboard. I leapt to her rescue and made a grab for her foot but it was too late. The next minute she was in the water and then under the water, probably getting mixed up in the propeller with no chance of getting her back on board. I looked down but she'd already disappeared from sight. All I could see was a lot of bubbles. One of the men came to lean over the back of the boat to see if he could see anything but explained there was little he could do and she was likely 'a gonner'.

I didn't enjoy the rest of the trip. All I could think about was Margarita: one minute – head back enjoying a leisurely boat trip, the next – turning backward somersaults and disappearing under a boat's propeller. It was all very unfortunate, and in a way, unfair, though you can't really blame the wind for your partner disappearing over the back of a boat. But I couldn't help thinking how – yet again – fate seemed to be against us.

But I'd been in a similar situation more than once and it's best to move on on these occasions rather than sitting around moping and feeling sorry for yourself. It was a savage blow to lose a partner in such circumstances. But I knew getting to the shop quickly might help in putting the whole unfortunate incident behind me.

When I got out of the boat I had a quick look round the back but there was nothing to see. As a parting gesture I tossed a pound coin in the river and made a wish.

Back at the shop the women were full of the fact I was back again. My luck was in. I was hoping there'd be a direct replacement, which proved to be the case. They asked what happened to Margarita-Three and when I explained she got caught in a gust of wind and disappeared over the back of a boat they shook their heads and seemed to be of a similar opinion that it had all been rather unfortunate.

But these things happen and with Margarita-Four ready and waiting on the shelf I was able to do a bit of mental adjusting – able to more or less pick up where we'd left off earlier that morning. Which more or less seemed to work. And is the way a lot of men are when their partners or wives part company. When one goes, another arrives on the scene to take her place.

The women in the shop said I needed to be more careful this time and maybe it would be fourth time lucky. I said 'let's hope so' and left with a new Margarita tucked firmly under my arm.

So – with Margarita-Four in-tow I arrived back at the flat and set about familiarising her with her new surroundings. She seemed to find it all quite agreeable and as a 'welcome home' gesture I took her to the bedroom and we made love – as the man at the sex-class would have put it...going at it *hammer and tongue* with the bed making all kinds of peculiar noises and Margarita coming out with some amazing vocabulary that, I have to admit, drove me to even greater heights. After which, neither of us had much energy for anything other than a quiet night in front of the tv.

Which was much the way our lives tended to be. We didn't see much of other people and I see nothing of my parents, neither of whom want anything to do with me. I once tried introducing them to Margarita but according to them I'm depraved and disgusting; an insult to the family's name and they made it clear as far as they are concerned, I don't exist. Which is a shame in a way, but like I said...there are some strange people around! My mother is a bit prim and proper and likes things done a certain way, and my father is very rich and has some successful businesses which I think are kept abroad so he avoids paying tax, which some people say is disgusting. Which just goes to show...one man's meat is another man's poison.

But it was a day when the warmer weather was upon us that things took an altogether unexpected turn...

It was one of those sunny days but without it being too hot that I decided a picnic in the countryside would be a good idea. I packed a few 'goodies' for lunch and we set off, needing to catch a few buses before we were away from built-up areas. We got a few funny looks on the bus which isn't unusual and one man taking a seat opposite looked up and said *Do me a fucking favour mate*...in a half joking, half sarcastic voice that could have spelt trouble but he got off after two stops.

Being out in the countryside was a welcome change. There were people around but it wasn't too busy and we found a nice spot close to some trees for a bit of privacy with a river close by. We had our lunch and I was of a mind to cuddle and kiss Margarita but decided against. I always think doing that sort of thing in public is a bit showy. Like you're saying...*Look at me everyone, I've got a partner.* Plus – it isn't really the sort of thing to be doing with other people not far away.

So we were leaning against a tree enjoying a bit of warmth but I had an urge to stretch my feet a little. Margarita seemed comfortable propped up against a tree and there was no-one around as far as I could see, so I thought it would be okay to have a stroll on my own for fifteen minutes or so.

I didn't go far. Just past a bend in the river and up the slope of a hill before setting off back to check Margarita was okay.

Even as I approached I sensed something wasn't quite right.

But it was when I got close, looking from behind a tree that despite the warm weather – I froze to the spot. For there was Margarita, on the grass lying on her back with a man virtually on top of her. There was no doubting what they were up to. Peeping between the branches I could see him kissing her and fondling her, at one point, his hand rising to caress one of her breasts. But the wide-eyed, rosy-cheeked expression on her face was enough to convince me what was happening wasn't solely down to him!

It was as much a painful as a shocking thing to be witnessing at close hand but worse still in that it was clear Margarita was making no effort to resist his advances; that she seemed to be content and happy to submit herself to him, as to me!

As well as shock, I felt my anger rising and decided enough was enough. I leapt out from behind the bush and was of a mind to challenge the man right there and then. But when he heard my exclamation...*Oi mate, what do you think you're up to?* He was suddenly on his feet and taking to his heels. I had the feeling he might have been doing the zip up on his trousers which annoyed me even more. He was soon off and out of sight and there was little to be gained from pursuing him. Aside from which, my anger was equally aimed at Margarita. It doesn't surprise me that men look at Margarita and find her attractive. But that doesn't give them the right to go ahead and take advantage. Nor does it mean Margarita ought to let them take advantage. What struck me was that for the first time, my anger was as much at her as at the man causing problems.

I walked back to where she was lying there looking a little puffed-up and full of herself. I didn't say anything because I couldn't see the point. Margarita isn't really one for making conversation. I just sat down at her side and thought for a moment, watching the river flowing only a matter of feet away and in an instant realised where I stood. That if such a thing could happen once, it could happen more than once. And that the idea of us picking up from where we'd left off before I went for a walk simply wasn't going to happen.

I gave her what might be described as a wistful look and she looked back. I think she knew she'd done wrong but knew equally that there was little she could do about it; like the river – it was all water under the bridge by now. I sensed those big eyes were, for once, looking quite sad, like she knew the game was up between us – but I wasn't to be deterred from what I knew I needed to do.

I carried her to the river and lowered her onto the surface of the water. I don't mind admitting there was a lump in my throat as I released her and gave her a gentle push, seeing her look me directly in the eye as she drifted into the main stream of the river, at which point she looked up, staring at the tops of trees and the sky. I watched her drift round the corner looking from that point and distance like a child's rubber dingy – and a minute or so later, disappear from sight.

I picked up my things and got back. It had been a severe blow and on arriving back in my flat I headed straight for the whisky bottle. Like the incident in the pub the anger was still there, but with a sense of frustration that was a new experience for me.

Given the circumstances I wasn't going to hang around and wait too long. I know some men, and women, are happy being on their own, but it's not really for me. I like a partner, a companion to share things with and be a part of my life. And I like sex on a regular basis. Partly because it's good for you and helps stop prostate cancer. Though they never tell you about that on tv. Instead they tell you about people going on marches and wearing badges in their lapels. Which is probably because in England no-one likes to talk about these things. Like we say...there are definitely some strange people about! It reminds me of a line a man at the sex-class used to come out with to get a laugh when we discussed such matters: *Shooting the sherbet once a week, keeps the pecker at its peak.*

Back at the shop the women seemed surprised.

'What...back again?' they said.

I wasn't going to explain. I didn't want them knowing the details, partly because they might feel some responsibility for Margarita's behaviour given they were the ones I'd got her from. I just said we'd 'had our differences' and left it at that.

They nodded, and – as they often do – exchanged looks. But there was a problem in that I'd bought the last of the Margaritas! They showed me one or two other possibilities: *Naughty Naomi* and *Lithesome Linda*. A third option...*Kiss Me Quick Cassandra* had been claimed by a man only the previous day. They showed me Naomi who had blonde curls and a very wide mouth like she was about to break into song or maybe scream.

She felt good and looked good. They showed me *Lithesome Linda* too, who was a little slimmer with smaller, quite narrow eyes like she had something on her mind she couldn't wait to tell you. It was strange to be looking at someone other than Margarita but, of course, there was nothing to stop me re-naming her once we got home. I left shortly after with *Naughty Naomi* tucked under my arm.

So – as the saying goes – hopefully fifth time lucky. We're getting on fine and with luck will continue to do so. As in the past we like to keep ourselves to ourselves and I suppose some people might think us a rather odd couple, but there is no reason for them to think that. They say people who are single, who don't have a partner, sometimes imagine a woman out there somewhere who – under different circumstances – might have been their partner, and wonder where she is, *who* she is and what she's like. Maybe Margarita's my way of answering those questions. I wondered about getting a dog but I wasn't sure how Margarita would feel about that. And it might get over excited and get its claws in her which could prove disastrous. Then I'd be back at the shop again and the women would say 'Not again!' And I'd nod and tell them how there'd been an unfortunate accident when the dog got too frisky with Margarita (or *Naughty Naomi*) and they'd nod and – not for the first time – exchange glances.

I'm wondering whether to go to Mave's classes again when they start up in September. She's doing a series of lessons on *Advanced Lovemaking – The Next Step* which could be interesting. I'm not quite sure what it means or what it involves but it could be worth giving it a go.

Which brings us back to pretty much where we started. Am I happy living as I do? I think so. I don't yearn for a great deal other than to enjoy life with my partner and despite a few ups and downs I can't complain about the way things have turned out. They say life's about making the most of whatever opportunities come your way. And if some people are a bit on the strange side, it's perhaps best to leave them to it. After all – the world's full of strange people. Maybe that's what makes it such an interesting place to live.

* * * * *

Notes

1 'Margarita'…'Call These Stories'.
2 'When Margarita Met Candice'…'Stories For Airports'

Café Au Lait

It was beneath the clear blue skies of an April morning but with still a bit of a chill in the air that, Peter Decroix – a regular at the café a few streets behind *Rue De La Forge*, one of the district's most frequented boulevards – sat nursing a coffee, whilst taking in what bit of sunlight manage to filter its way over the rooftops opposite. As a relative newcomer to these shores he'd rather taken to this part of town, the cobbled streets and shabby facades – a perfect antidote to the show-biz glitz and glamour of thoroughfares only a kilometre or so away.

A patisserie at the end of the street was one of only two other businesses in evidence. The other, a second café on the opposite side of the street about fifty metres away – a less appealing place; its interior largely hidden behind canopies, its patio obscured from direct sunlight for much of the day, a more subdued establishment on all fronts in terms of any regular day-time trade.

The street was even quieter than usual. A bubble-car appearing and quickly disappearing, a cat crossing the street and disappearing through the cat-flap of a building opposite were noteworthy events. The café owner – sensing little else was likely to disturb his morning – doing his usual trick of disappearing from sight the minute Decroix had taken his seat.

A matter of little concern to Delcroix. He had his newspaper, his coffee which – in time-honoured fashion – would go largely untouched. The only hint of a disturbance, a lorry-river's expressions of frustration at attempting to reverse his vehicle into one of the narrower streets a few blocks away.

And – around five minutes after taking his seat – the sound of raised voices somewhere to his right, appearing to come from inside the cafe further down the street. Glancing casually, he sought refuge in his paper, no way seeking to involve himself in matters that were – and would continue to be – none of his business.

An understandable line to adopt, if not so easy to adhere to, when the voices – once contained within the confines of the café – suddenly appeared as rants spilling onto the patio and then onto the pavement itself.

The argument was between a woman – a beefy-looking woman with black hair tied in a bun and in keeping with current fashion, wearing elbow length white gloves. Her combatant – a spindly bespectacled figure: the kind you'd imagine doing everything in his power to avoid physical confrontations rather than seeking to involve himself in them.

Decroix shook his newspaper – a show of irritation at being obliged to witness such carryings-on, if only from fifty or so metres distance. Fortunately, a line of bushes did a pretty good job of concealing him from view beyond the patio close to the pavement, his inclination – as is common-ground on such occasions – to make a show of ignoring the interruption whilst privately condemning the antics of folk who really ought to know better.

On two occasions the man went as far as to make a grab for the woman, once by the hair, and then later, thrusting her against a metal post at the side of the patio. Eventually forcing her over the table, at which point the woman had cried out, appearing to genuinely fear for her safety.

A development Decroix had even less urge to be viewing at such close quarters and had him thinking maybe a swift exit might be on the cards. Or a venture indoors to find the café-owner who possibly knew the pair and might be in a position to step in and calm the waters before things got totally out of hand.

More shouts followed, the swipe of an arm as the man lashed out and the woman reeled and sank back onto a table. A more piercing cry as, moments later, with a glance along both sides of the street – the man appeared to reach for something in his pocket.

It was in the split-second that followed that the woman reached down to make a grab at something to the left of the table, raising it above the man now crouched above her before bringing it down somewhere at the base of his spine. As a result of which – he fell, rolled a few times and then appeared to lie still by one of the tables.

Delcroix instinctively looked away. And had common sense prevailed he'd have gone the whole hog and moved himself away – in so doing, avoiding the spectacle of the woman rising from her seat to begin pacing round the body, and on looking repeatedly along both sides of the street – bring the object repeatedly into contact with the man's upper half, after which she backed-off and with another quick glance in both directions, knelt to the floor.

Delcroix stiffened in his seat. Aside from it being as unsightly a means of settling an argument as he'd seen in some time – all fingers were pointing at him being the sole witness, a prospect that: both in the present, and in whatever context might follow – he'd have few qualms about avoiding.

Thoughts interrupted by further movement on the patio.

Delcroix watched the woman reach for the man's ankles, and on making doubly sure there was no-one around – aside from herself and the man she currently held by the feet – drag the body to a spot close to the street, leave him a moment and then turn to a large metal manhole cover, lifting it with some effort and placing it to one side. After which, she was back to reaching for his ankles and pulling him along the ground until – with a final glance along both sides of the street – she slid him with a heave of ample-sized shoulders into the hole in the ground which – once he'd slipped from sight to his presumed resting-place several metres beneath the street – she immediately covered with the metal lid, dragging it across and securing it in place.

Seconds later she was back to the table checking for any tell-tale stains on the patio before taking her seat, lighting a cigarette and raising the gloved fingers of each hand to check for evidence that might warrant their removal from the scene at the earliest opportunity.

From his still relatively secure position semi-concealed behind a line of privet hedges Delcroix sought to keep what was happening – or *had* happened – in some kind of perspective.

His luck was in, in so far as she didn't appear to have spotted him, and so long as he kept his wits about him he was reasonably sure the plan he'd been working on would suffice in rescuing him from potential further involvement: to allow sufficient time to lapse before rising casually from his seat, newspaper tucked under his arm to head nonchalantly in the opposite direction, and thus pick up his day from where he'd left it only a half hour or so ago.

Thoughts interrupted by further activity: a man, presumably the cafe owner, dressed in a long striped apron, joining the woman on the patio and then on the street, following her indicating in both directions with a raised arm, before returning to his business indoors.

Above all else, Delcroix knew the need to pick his moment. Timing his departure only as and when things had calmed to a point of him either being ignored or perceived to be a passer-by with little call or reason to be interfering in matters that didn't concern him.

Another option – perhaps the most practical and public-spirited in most people's book – to hail the café-owner, fill him in on what had happened and get him to inform the appropriate authorities immediately – and *then* disappear from the scene.

Except – everyone knew that wasn't the way it worked. He'd been a witness. Probably the *only* witness (except for the woman and maybe the café owner – and possibly the individual viewing proceedings from a few metres beneath the street). In light of which – confirmation as to what had occurred prior to their arrival and what might transpire as a result of it, would rest largely on his shoulders. A fact the police were unlikely to overlook simply by way of doing him a favour.

Which begged the question – what *exactly* had occurred? A woman at the point of being assaulted who had acted out of self-defence by smacking her assailant with a large, as yet unidentified object, before ditching him in a hole in the ground. The rights and wrongs of which were hardly his concern. He wasn't a policeman or a lawyer – he was a member of the public attempting to pass time over a cup of coffee and a read of his newspaper.

It was on returning from paying his dues in a box left on the counter with a view to making a swift, hopefully not too conspicuous exit, that he was aware of a further development: a figure half crouched and looking all too conspicuous on the pavement opposite.

Looking up, he caught the eye of the woman who – for whatever reason – had seen fit to abandon her seat in the café to occupy a spot crouched against the wall of the building opposite – in Delcroix's immediate firing line – staring him directly in the eye.

Again Delcroix's instinct was to look elsewhere. Whatever had led to the woman upping herself from what had been a position of relative safety – to all intents nothing had changed. He still had no more to do with these people's bizarre antics than when he'd first taken his seat. And the sooner the woman grasped the fact instead of sitting there skulking against the wall – the better.

A line of thinking clear enough on one side of the street, though apparently less so on the pavement opposite. Where moments later – almost as if timed to coincide with Delcroix's mounting impatience – the woman sank to her knees, buried her head in her hands, and dissolved in floods of tears.

Delcroix looked over his shoulder. There was still no sight of the cafe owner, though whether his appearance would prove to be in anyone's interests at this juncture was debatable.

Still resolved to viewing the situation through an objective if – by this stage – not entirely dispassionate eye, he watched the woman clearly in a state of some distress – no doubt seeing Delcroix's presence and subsequent intervention as set to seal her fate in a way she could hardly have bargained on back on the café patio.

A prospect Delcroix wasn't inclined to dwell on to any great extent aside from a possible second option that might yet save the day – on both sides of the street.

Though not yet fluent in the language he was keen to improve – and reasonably sure he could get her to get her to see that though he'd witnessed the scenario from the beginning (aside from the bit indoors) it was clear to anyone that she'd acted out of self-defence. Which meant that as far as anyone – particularly the police – were concerned, he'd seen absolutely nothing. He'd stress the *nothing*. Adding that – if ever questioned in court he wouldn't have the faintest idea what anyone was talking about. And, as such, she would have no cause to worry on his count.

All in all, a risky tactic – but hardly one likely to backfire on him. He'd have done his bit and the rest would be down to her.

Crossing the road he had a quick run-through of how to begin so as to make things clear from the start. Hopefully avoiding the woman making a run for it before he'd even opened his mouth to speak.

Stepping onto the pavement he saw the woman looking curiously in his direction...

'Look...*let me explain something...*' he began____

On concluding his speech there was little evidence the woman had grasped a word he'd been saying or at least the intention behind it. Her initial response...to back herself further against the wall. Only then relaxing sufficiently to look him more firmly in the eye, before finally extending a hand. Indication that what he'd been saying *had* finally hit home – but given her distraught state – had simply needed time to register.

Seizing his hand she urged him to join her in retracing her steps to the café patio.

It was Delcroix's turn to hold back, further involvement of whatever the woman had in mind – pretty much the last thing on *his* mind. Yet the woman was adamant. He'd done her a huge favour which was not to be shrugged off with a few exchanges on a pavement. Aside from which, this was some grip the woman had – to a point that attempting to shake her loose might prove more problematical than simply going along with whatever token of esteem might be heading his way.

Leading him to the café she insisted he take a seat. On taking a seat opposite and still visibly shaken, she directed his eye to a spot beneath the table where a metal object resembling a horseshoe was lying as if waiting to be discovered. Delcroix got her point. That given the events of the last half hour she was reluctant to go anywhere near the offending object that on closer examination seemed to be some kind of metal doorstop, probably in use when the café was in full swing.

If only to hurry proceedings along, there'd be no problem taking the thing to the side of the patio where – the woman was quick to explain – it would be temporarily discarded before being driven by the café owner to a more permanent home at the bottom of the nearest lake.

It was on returning to his seat that she rose from her seat and went into the cafe where seconds later, the man in the striped apron emerged alongside her, the pair crossing the floor to Delcroix, who – on being rapturously received on both sides – was urged to remain in his place where – following another, slightly lengthier trip to the counter – brandies were to be the delivered, courtesy of the house.

It was a lively, if not altogether welcomed affair. And no huge surprise when – on emptying the glasses for what might have been the third or fourth time – the pair took to embracing unashamedly in the middle of the patio.

Certainly less a surprise than a few moments later – when the scream of car engines alongside a string of flashing blue lights came to a halt just as the pair broke from their clinch, still hugging each other and pointing in Delcroix's direction.

Within seconds four policemen had leapt from the car.

What followed would be difficult to recall. Delcroix aware only of being grabbed from behind, the woman and the café-owner continuing to cling to each other whilst pointing repeatedly at Delcroix and at the manhole-cover a few metres away.

And moments later – of doors opening and slamming and being bundled into the rear seat, handcuffed whilst desperately trying to make himself heard – and understood.

'*Look...let me explain something...*' he began.

'All in good time sir,' one of the uniformed officers had said. 'All in good time.'

* * * *

On An Island

A teacher, twenty seven years of age with a mass of lank black hair picked himself from the grounded dinghy whilst attempting to blink salt, sun and bits of sand from his eyes. He looked left, right and then straight ahead where a forest of trees appeared to run the length of coastline to a point where it did an about turn, bordered by a series of rock crevices. The dinghy had fortunately made it in one piece.

As his foot made contact with the sea-bed, a girl with chestnut hair eased her way over the side to join him. With his mind beginning to clear, he waited for her, watching her wade through the final few feet of water to his side of the dinghy.

'Okay?' It was the first word either had spoken since drawing to a halt. She nodded, reaching to grip his hand, the other hand raised to sweep strands of hair from her eyes.

It was hot. Stiflingly hot. Something both would need time to get used to. And even at this point had their clothes: in her case, a short skirt and sleeveless top; in his case, tee-shirt and knee length shorts – saturated within minutes.

On finding herself on solid ground, the girl looked round, evidently in a state of some confusion. At some point – and with some justification – he'd imagined events would catch up with her and that there'd be tears. And this might well be the time for it to happen. But thus far, it hadn't happened. She hadn't cried. Instead, she'd continued to watch him, following his every move. Wanting to be a part of whatever the next few hours, maybe days held in store for the pair of them. Watching him make his way back to the dinghy, reaching for the first of three crates, the other two drawn into position for later.

'Come on, we need to move.' He was aware of the need to keep busy, to keep themselves occupied. The more they found to do, the better. The girl responded, again reaching for his hand, the other hand steadying herself against a waterline reaching to a few inches below her skirt.

Ensuring the dinghy was firmly beached against the sea-bed, he led the way.

It was on releasing his grip that the girl stopped a moment, finally mustering the courage to return to the events of the previous day. Recollections of which were vague – aside from a scene of pandemonium on-deck midst a crescendo of activity, at the time almost unbearable to be witnessing. And moments later – people piling on top of her.

All of which would be put on hold – for a while at least.

Partly in so far as he knew as little, or possibly even less than she did. The entire episode passing with him temporarily unconscious on the deck of the ship.

He looked from whence they'd come – cradling his eyes against the sky, giving an impression that what they were both seeking was out there somewhere, waiting to be discovered. But, for now – beyond vision.

'What happened?' His thoughts were interrupted by a voice on the far side of the dinghy. Though innocently put and an obvious enough question to ask, there would be no immediate response. Whatever viable explanation might be at hand would have to wait a while. Whilst difficult if not impossible to put too far behind them.

It had been on regaining consciousness in the dinghy he'd presumably been pushed into – possibly on the grounds of them hailing from the same school party – that he'd immediately identified the other occupant as Kim Partington – a Year Eleven pupil in his GCSE English class; one of the official party of forty five pupils from their school.

He'd crept over to her, finding her lying still but breathing and on initial inspection, not appearing to bear any visible injuries. Of the others, he knew nothing and would gain little by trying to draw any conclusions. The *only* conclusion that mattered: that with whoever's aid – he'd survived, along with the girl – and as a consequence both had been granted some chance of survival though for how long and in what circumstances remained to be seen. Which, for now, was *all* that mattered. Fifteen minutes later the girl had stirred but only briefly. He'd leave her. The last thing he needed at that moment was for her to have any firm grasp of what was happening.

Having drifted for what felt like days but was in reality no more than seven to eight hours, the sight of land was a huge relief – but also a source of some concern. He'd had no way of knowing their position and no way of anticipating what to expect once they arrived on whatever shores they appeared to be heading for.

On approaching the coastline there were more rocks and more dunes, huge creepers and trees with palm-like leaves designed to cut out a good fifty percent of sunlight.

He was back to the dinghy, needing to remind himself of the next step: to make use of available time before it got dark, whenever that would be. Which meant leaving the dinghy. It would hopefully come to no harm semi-submerged on the sand.

With some urgency he led her onto dry land, their surroundings – even at such close quarters – passing virtually without comment.

Fifty yards beyond the sand it was noticeably warmer. Several paths had emerged alongside the vegetation, or if not literally paths – clearings that would serve as thoroughfares if required.

They had successfully hauled themselves up a steady incline, picking their way through brambles and an assortment of tangled vegetation, largely weeds and strange twenty foot growths with huge drooping leaves.

Still few words were spoken. Just warnings to avoid tripping or stumbling – warnings she had already been quick to heed.

It was on shading his eyes that he'd spotted a cave-like hole in a face of rock some twenty yards away at the head of the next incline.

It warranted investigation. And three or four minutes later, the opportunity to sit in more than welcome shade, brushing themselves down and without necessarily intending it – allowing brief acknowledgement of a stroke of good fortune. It was a larger space than he'd imagined, stretching thirty to forty feet into the heart of the rock. He crept along its perimeter, breathing the relatively cool, slightly musty air – feeling his way for sharp plants or gaps in the surface.

The girl left him a moment to check the area around the entrance, cupping her eye to look back on the short distance from the beach.

Inside, a layer of coarse grass covering the ground was examined thoroughly if only to establish its credentials to serve as a kind of base. Somewhere to put the stuff from the dingy and return to later, if and when necessary. He called her inside, inviting her to take a look, watching her stepping in tiny circles, still some way from getting any sort of grasp on what was happening.

She watched him tend to a crate, two bottles of water promptly placed on the ground along with what appeared to be two small packs of biscuits.

A period of drinking and eating followed. There were curranty bits in the biscuits making them a bit more palatable and, on checking, plenty more bottles where the first two had come from. But with a reminder that they would need to go easy. The consumption of water, just one of many things requiring careful management over the next few day at least.

As reward for her exertions the girl allowed herself a moment's repose, falling back on her haunches, her skirt rising to permit some degree of ventilation. She stared at the short distance they'd covered from the sea; the bracken and masses of undergrowth less formidable once en-route from the dingy. Both guessed it was mid-afternoon, though it would only be a guess. Such things as morning and afternoon already seemed largely meaningless. Better to gauge things from the sun making its way across the sky where it met a thin haze drifting in from the sea.

He took advantage of the pause to view his companion more closely: a sixteen year-old suburban London schoolgirl whose world – in the course of twenty-four hours – had been turned on its head. Yet – perhaps thankfully – without it appearing to have fully registered. He recalled a condition he thought might be *Involuntary Amnesia*: the mind and body going into lockdown following occasions of extreme trauma. That maybe that was something to do with it. Though at school she'd been quick to know where the common-ground between kids and the teachers stopped. A consideration, as a teacher he was equally aware of. Whilst also aware – back to the present – that beyond simply putting what had happened out of their mind, something far bigger awaited. Quite what that was would – for now – remain a mystery.

Reason enough for focusing solely on the task in hand.

He helped her to her feet, allowing her a moment to brush her skirt and seize a bottle of water. Placing it in small canvas bag found in one the crates. It was far too hot to be wearing a top and a skirt. Spare clothing was hidden in one of the crates but digging it out and changing into whatever it consisted of at this time of day made little sense.

Leaving the cave, they began making their way up the hill, Kim reaching for assistance in finding her feet over the first few yards of rock.

'Sir....' He waited for her to draw level before calling her to a halt – quietly reassuring her (and without any trace of a teacher-like voice) that things were different now and would be until they got back home. That the rules of school didn't need to apply here. That she didn't need to address him as *sir.* That his name was Dave as she probably knew anyway.

She looked up from scuffing the ground with her foot. He got the impression she was trying not to smile. It was a fact that most of the pupils, particularly the older pupils knew *all* the teachers' names. Especially the younger male teachers. He asked her what she'd been about to say. Whatever it was appeared to have been forgotten.

'Okay...let's keep moving,' he said.

They reached a spot awarding a view of the sea in a near three-hundred-and sixty degree arc beneath them. Confirmation they were on an island. The implications of which were no clearer than when they'd first arrived. They stepped further, taking care not to lose track of the route they'd followed from the cave.

The heat was almost suffocating, effectively weighing down their every step. Kim pulling repeatedly at the top, looking to where several hours sweat had left its mark in long brown steaks reaching from her shoulder to just above her breasts. He could sympathise but offer little by way of practical assistance. A change of clothes would be possible once back at the cave. But even then it would be better to wait a while.

Though he couldn't be sure, his initial impression – that the island was uninhabited – seemed to be confirmed. There'd been no signs of life aside from insects and the odd scurrying noises from the trees. And looking down the far side of the slope, the sea was, from where they were standing, no more than a quarter mile away. A whole stretch of coastline awaiting investigation the following day. It was difficult to focus on too many things at once. Getting an idea of the general layout and geography had been their initial aim. They took a moment to drink. Small amounts as opposed to lengthy swallows. He watched her take short sips from the bottle, instantly re-capping it to avoid waste.

'So if it's an island does that mean it might be more difficult to be rescued?' For once he'd hesitate before answering.

He shook his head. All he could say for certain was that they were possibly hundreds of miles from the nearest land. A part of the world meaning little to her, or maybe anyone; a vast expanse likely littered with dots of land too insignificant to feature on even the most detailed map. It wasn't the moment to be contemplating such issues. They had the cave to return to and, later – food to tend to. With the nights sleeping arrangements to follow.

The three *Emergency Survival Crates* had been lifted from the dinghy to be hauled in shifts to a halfway point before tackling the last hike to the cave. On arrival the contents of each were awarded due attention: tinned food, dried milk, utensils, a mini-stove with three replacement cartridges. Toiletries and a medical box. All neatly packed, tagged and listed item by item. On the food side were three boxes of dried biscuit-like rusks – vacuum sealed. What space remained, packed with tea and coffee and emergency clothing.

On returning to the cave his advice to save the change of clothing until later was heeded. What they hadn't yet done was investigate the area close to the cave. A task best undertaken before the skies began darkening. How long dusk lasted in these parts could only be guessed at. His impression – if Mediterranean holidays were anything to go by – possibly sinking into darkness the moment the sun disappeared from view.

To the left a fairly steep descent led to a stretch of sandy ground. They helped each other, stepping onto a plateau and disappearing into a thicket of trees coming face to face with a crag jutting from a rock face and on taking a few steps further – hearing a noise that could only be water falling somewhere close by. The flowers and denser undergrowth giving way to vines that were much thicker; thicker, greener and unless he was mistaken, damper.

They struggled through a gap between two boulders. Then looked up. They were looking at a waterfall – or what could loosely be classed as a waterfall: a steady stream tumbling from a spot too high to identify from where they were standing. A sight that had them stepping closer, following the movement of water from the top of the ridge round a corner to their left. Rounding a bend they came face to face with a tiny pool, maybe five feet wide. Not deep, maybe a foot or two feet in parts. They eased their way past another jutting piece of rock. From which point they could watch the water tumbling from above, striking the pool a pattern of concentric circles. The obvious question...Was it drinkable? They stepped closer. Releasing his hand Kim was already stepping round the pool, trying to convince herself it was real. Looking for permission to do what she'd been aching to do since first spotting it. To kneel down and douse head, shoulders, arms – splashing the stuff any part of her that could comfortably be reached.

It was okay, but he warned her not to drink just yet. He joined her, reaching to splash water onto his face and neck. Though not quite so enthusiastically – aware of the need not to be seen going overboard about things. He cupped a hand in the stream just before it reached the pool. It tasted fine – virtually tasteless. He looked across and nodded.

Back at the cave there was plenty to occupy them. Kim delving through one of the crates to find items of clothing that might see her through the following day. She'd found a pair of shorts and a low-neck sleeveless top, holding them at shoulder-height for his reaction. He assured her they'd do fine. She shook the shorts and placed them to one side.

The evening was soon upon them. Opportunity for a change of clothing and a more leisurely trip to the pool. He watched her make her way down the slope clutching a flannel, towel and a change of clothing in one hand, the other arm extended as an aid to keeping her balance as she stepped towards the first line of trees.

'Be careful,' he shouted after her. The first time she'd ventured anywhere on her own. But she was probably already too far down the slope to hear him. He returned to the canisters of gas, having the cooking-ring and cartridges to sort out and cans of whatever they'd be eating for supper.

Her temporary absence was a reminder, if one was needed, of how his responsibilities had changed, taking the pair of them into entirely unchartered territory. But he was reasonably sure he had her trust, which – without ever seeking confirmation – would hopefully continue to be the case. Thankfully she was a good kid. Quieter and more introverted than some. But that wasn't a problem; a side of some kids he actually found quite endearing. And – as if to prove the theory that you often got to know more about the kids away from the classroom – he'd already seen a steely side to her. And in circumstances no-one her age could – or should – be expected to have to cope with.

He turned to the rear of the cave where two light-weight sleeping-bags had been put to one side for later.

Shortly after, she was back – the towel hung over a tree to dry. She brushed her top, pulling the sleeveless tee-shirt and stepping from the mouth of the cave.

'Okay?'

'Good. Quite warm.' She turned, pulling the lightweight cotton top to exaggerate its loose fitting. 'What do you think?'

'Terrific,' he said, reaching for his own clothing before getting to his feet.

He'd managed to master the technique for washing in what proved to be an extremely confined space. It felt strange, not just to be wallowing around outdoors in a pool of tepid water – but with one of his pupils only a stone's throw away. But both knew it was simply the circumstances they'd found themselves in. And that it would be foolish not to take advantage of such a discovery. Particularly with there being no viable alternative. Nor that it mattered in either case. The chance of a bit of privacy something both were happy to take advantage of.

Getting a meal together had been next on the agenda. She'd watched the process of emptying the contents in turn into a pan to be heated on a single ring. A few plastic plates and cutlery were included, removed from their plastic wallets whilst she examined the space outside the cave's entrance from a seating point of view.

Whilst eating they'd talked. Only once was the issue of their rescue raised. He still avoided making it a topic of conversation, his knowledge of how these things worked – as sketchy as his knowing their exact location. The island probably insignificant in terms of 'identifiable-land' on computer screens. Whether mobile phones would have been of any aid he couldn't be sure and, in any case, would be entirely academic. He'd never owned a mobile-phone – much to his pupils' amusement. And Kim's Smartphone had gone missing on-board ship. Again, something she hadn't yet commented on – unusual for one her age. Though, as far as he was concerned, the best way for it to stay.

Only once did they return to events on-board ship. It was difficult talking about it. The explosion and everything stemming from it serving only to prompt questions, the answers to which would serve no real purpose. What mattered was that they were alive. With every chance of that continuing to be the case – for a while at least.

One thing she hadn't mentioned was her family. He knew something of her circumstances and that it wasn't an altogether happy tale. The story went that her father had been convicted of some fraudulent act at work though whether he was in custody he wasn't sure. It wasn't the sort of detail routinely disclosed to staff. Her mother too had had her problems. There'd been talk of drug issues though again it was difficult to know the facts. The nature of her relationship with her parents, particularly her mother never being entirely clarified. At school it wasn't deemed appropriate to raise such issues unless they appeared to affect a pupil's work. And then only through the appropriate channels.

It was some time after taking their seats on the grass that with a little prompting – and feet drawn contemplatively to be gripped in both arms – she felt it appropriate to reveal some details: how her father was in prison, the exact nature of his crime not entirely clear to her beyond it being something to do with an issue at work. And how her mother had been struggling with depression and was currently on what she thought was called a drug management…She corrected herself but couldn't remember the word…rehab__ course. 'Rehabilitation'. He helped her with the word.

Possibly cushioned by distance, she talked without trace of emotion or seeking sympathy. The overriding impression – the chance to distance herself from it all, almost a relief without call or cause to be over dramatic.

She had stopped speaking.

What followed was the hopefully more straightforward matter of trying to get a reasonable night's sleep. He'd no way of knowing how it was going to pan-out. He hoped, for her sake, it wouldn't be too much of an issue – the pair of them under the one roof and in such close proximity. Both were physically and emotionally drained from the events of the last twenty-four hours and the routine for settling down had already been established. She'd get herself organised first. Once settled and with the candles extinguished, he'd join her back inside.

In the semi-darkness little more was said. It wasn't particularly comfortable. But both knew these things would take time.

Settled inside their sleeping-bags he checked if she was okay. She nodded, turning to face him for what would be the last time that day.

He woke – for some reason surprised to see her already up and around.

'Tea?' She looked over her shoulder, tea-bags at the ready.

She gave the impression of having had a reasonable night's sleep. He watched her tend to a can of dried milk and two plastic cups. Pleased and relieved to see her relatively upbeat mood was still in evidence. She strode across the floor, leaning to take two biscuits from one of the crates. His suggestion following breakfast that they investigate the other side of the island seemed to meet her approval.

Leaving the cave armed with water and a canvas bag, first stop was the ridge. The heat slowed them at times to a crawl, enabling them to pick up the pace only along the flatter stretches where the grass grew thinner, possibly stunted by the long-term effects of the sun. Only on the steeped descents did they return to helping each other over tree stumps and tangles of roots that were a trickier proposition than their side of the island. Some leaves almost the size of dustbin lids.

It was on reaching a flatter surface with a bit more space to play with, that they stumbled on an area of small trees, each bearing bluish purple fruit about the size of plums, for him just about reachable stood on tip-toe. He took one and handed it to her for examination, scouring the ground for signs of dead fruit littered with insects – some indication as to whether they'd be safe to eat. He wandered further but found nothing, returning to find her chewing eagerly and on his arrival, dropping what remained of the fruit to the ground. His gestures spoke plainly enough. As did hers: a finger drawn to her lips – her mouth opened to reveal lines of perfect teeth and a tongue extended for his inspection.

He took the joke, returning to the fruit hanging from the lowest branches. The chance of adding in a little fresh fruit to their diet was worth investigating but they'd need to play safe. They'd leave it for now. They knew where the trees were and could return as and when required. They took a couple to be put outside the cave as bait for insects or birds, possibly returning later.

With the left side of the island virtually covered, they took a detour to the sea – the one part of the island where he still felt uneasy. A feeling he couldn't easily explain following their detailed exploration of the place, other than reflecting on the fact that it was a remote part of the world in which they'd found themselves and though ninety-nine per-cent sure they were alone, it wasn't the sort of thing you could be absolutely sure about – the idea of advertising themselves in the wide open spaces doing little to ease his apprehension.

Reservations no way shared by Kim.

He watched her forge ahead along a strip of beach close to the water's edge. Putting sufficient distance between them before stopping to face him.

With the ocean as a backdrop – hair reaching almost to her waist – she reached down, releasing buttons, and with what remained of the next wave disintegrating around her ankles – stepped out of the shorts, taking a few steps back to deposit them on dry land before continuing her way, underwear-clad. Minutes later warming to the feel of water encircling her like a hoopla. And then she was under, instantly disappearing from view.

He watched – content to keep an eye on proceedings from the shade of nearby trees. The shorts – in his case – destined to remain firmly in-place.

It was fifteen minutes later that he watched her emerge from the shallows to occupy a spot not far from where he was sitting, the shorts lifted from their place on the sand to be held in front of her as she moved into the shade a few feet away. He did the diplomatic thing by looking away as she re-donned the shorts, standing to shake strands of soaking wet hair. Looking back to catch her doing up the buttons – in the process unable to avoid the sight of her breasts beneath the soaking top.

'Okay?' he asked, feeling slightly foolish at being slow to take advantage of one of the island's obvious attractions.

She nodded, reaching behind to straighten her top and then turning to begin retracing their steps.

Back at the cave the fruit was placed in the entrance area and a few feet away on the edge of the dip towards the pool. With a supply of water no longer an issue, two of the bottles had already been filled. Her task whilst he tended to the bottle filling – to investigate the medical box to check what ailments were catered for. Stomach sickness and bites came out top of the list. Along with water purifying tablets and a host of plasters, bandages and paracetamols.

Within half an hour the experiment seemed to have worked – handfuls of insects only too happy to take advantage of fruit not only laid on the ground but opened in readiness for them to partake as and when they fancied. Whether it *really* proved anything he couldn't be sure, but you could only take caution so far, and a few bites were hardly likely to prove fatal. They tasted good, if anything, sweeter than the plums at home. But it would still be wise not to overdo it. Stomach issues they could well do without.

Returning to get stocked-up on a few seemed as good a way as any of spending the next half hour, taking a slightly different route from the ridge. He offered to go alone but she wasn't in the mood to be left behind. Nor to leave him to his own devices just yet.

They retraced their steps from earlier and on returning to the highest point, took a more direct route towards the beach. If anything the going was tougher than before. Twice she hesitated, rescued by hands hauling her to a spot where she stood a moment – brushing herself down, paying particular attention to a number of tiny scratch marks an inch or so above each knee.

On returning to the trees she held the bag as he reached to take enough plums – if that's what they were – to last a couple of days. There'd be every chance of discovering more but they could wait till later.

What remained of the afternoon was spent investigating closer to the cave, an attempt to spot whatever wildlife might be lurking somewhere in the bushes: inhabitants of the island – assuming they existed – thus far proving to be extremely elusive. He was reminded of a book still in regular use with the GCSE pupils: *Lord Of The Flies* with its pig head impaled on a post – wondering how Kim would warm to the task of pursuing a 'beast' with a pointed stick before facing the task of separating its head from its shoulders. For close to an hour they wandered semi-aimlessly, spotting nothing aside from insects, birds and a few unidentified creatures occasionally hopping from branch to branch near the tops of trees.

Winding up close to the beach they returned to the dinghy. Only once had they re-visited it since their arrival. It was important for it to remain visible, hopefully to some extent from the air. And attempting to manoeuvre it or deflate it for whatever reason, could be a stupid move, even if they figured out how to go about it. It was unlikely to be a case of simply pulling out a few stoppers.

They'd headed to where it sat semi-submerged exactly as they'd left it, doing a quick check beneath the seating and in the cubby-hole at the front to check for any implements or tools that might previously have been overlooked, including flares or other devices designed to draw attention from a distance. But quickly establishing that the cupboard – as they say (in this case quite literally) – was bare.

Back at the cave the first knockings of evening were soon upon them. Their second day with no sign of rescue on the horizon. Not for the first time he regretted not having a mobile-phone. Not because it would necessarily work in their favour, but on the off chance it might. Giving some signal that could be picked up on-board ship somewhere close by. It was the lack of any communication that left him feeling helpless. Urging him to look out to sea every chance he got. Only once had Kim mentioned her Smartphone, and then only to recall where it had been when she'd been thrown to the floor, thinking it might have been on the table that was swept aside along with everything else in the vicinity. But it was the last she'd said about it and he wasn't going to raise the issue with her. Whether she'd know anything about mobile-phone reception halfway round the world was questionable and, in any case, wasn't going to get them anywhere. He'd wondered if she secretly resented the fact he didn't carry a phone like most men his age – guys sufficiently at home with the technology that, in current circumstances, might give sufficient signals to have the rescue planes on the scene within hours. Though even then there was no guarantee it wouldn't have suffered the same fate as hers. And whatever thoughts she had on the subject she was keeping entirely to herself.

Approaching the end of their second day with the bulk of the exploration behind them it was clear that for however long they'd be on the island – a couple of days, possibly longer – they'd have a fair amount of (what they'd come to call at school) 'downtime' to deal with. Times when they'd need to find stuff to keep them occupied; something barely warranting consideration back at home where time comes and quickly goes with barely the flick of an eyelid. But if he'd learnt anything in the last few days, it was the value of respecting the passing of each and every hour on return to their normal lives. Whether it would be the same with Kim was impossible to say; ideas it wasn't easy to exchange views on given her age.

They'd discovered sketch pads in one of the crates, along with pens and coloured pencils. He assumed they'd been included for writing messages or listing jobs needing to be addressed. But he now realised it was also a way of passing time. He'd noticed she'd taken to drawing. Which was a good thing to be doing. And didn't involve her wandering off on her own, which he'd still feel uneasy about. It wasn't that she was helpless or incapable. If anything very much the opposite, but he guessed it was the same as on the beach. That essentially – for all their increasing familiarity with the place – this was still alien territory: a temporary home they could never be one-hundred-per-cent sure about. And an environment hugely different from their own. That wandering off alone would inevitably involve some degree of risk, if only needing to negotiate the, at times, near-impenetrable undergrowth. Plus – the added factor of her being a girl. A striking looking girl at that.

Around the same time as the previous day they took turns washing at the pool. An arrangement that seemed to work okay first time round and they saw no reason to change. She'd go first while he got the stuff ready to eat. They'd agreed to stick to one meal a day in the evening and survive on biscuits and some of the rye bread-like stuff kept in polythene seals and fruit during the day. With no fussing about what they ate. An agreement reached to take turns in deciding which of the tins should be opened.

After eating she was back to her pictures. He'd have been interested to see what she'd been drawing but thought it best to do the diplomatic thing by keeping his distance – allowing her a bit of space without having someone peering over her shoulder.

It was fifteen minutes into her endeavours that she shuffled across to show him: a steep incline with a large oval shape half way up, bordered by what he took to be sea on one side and the sky above. She asked for an opinion. He told her he liked it. She'd let it go at that, but not without giving him one of her looks that suggested she'd been looking for a more critical reaction. He assured her she'd captured *the mood* of the first day down to a tee. Which – on returning to her spot – would suffice for the time being.

With the business of eating behind them and having cleared the air on *her* family details – she took the opportunity to ask about his. The kind of stuff the kids at school were interested to know about but weren't always sufficiently confident to ask about. She asked if he was married. He saw no reason to evade the question – or to lie. He told her he was single. And lived in a flat. And did the ordinary, unspectacular things most single men his age did. Which, as an answer – and as with the picture – would do for now. She'd been on the brink of asking whether he had a girlfriend but held back from asking, thinking maybe that would be a step too far. Even in present circumstances it wouldn't he right to be asking about that kind of thing.

Though it didn't stop him asking her about boyfriends. Perhaps teachers could take a few more liberties in that department. At school the older girls talked about boys ninety-per-cent of the time and girls like Kim rarely had problems attracting boys. She either had – or *chose* to have – little to say on the subject, her concentration deliberately focused more on adding a few more touches to the drawing.

'One or two,' she'd said, and left it at that. 'Nothing special.' She was back to the sketch-pad, raising it for him to comment.

She'd persisted in her habit of addressing him as *sir*. And each time he'd pulled her up on it. But it wasn't as simple as he'd suggested. Time-honoured traditions such as addressing teachers as *sir* or *miss* weren't easy to cast-off, and brought a sense of security. Even now, under such circumstances – these things continued to be important. Talking with her friends back at school was different. Then...they always used the teachers' first names.

But he was quite happy to talk about it. She knew his name was...Dave Davies. Designed to trip easily off the tongue. When she asked him about it he explained how his father had been a fan of The Kinks. Which meant nothing to her aside from showing some surprise, prompting the question...'Was he kinky?' He'd explained that The Kinks were a band. Or a *pop group* as they used to be called, from the 60's. And his favourite song was *Death Of A Clown*.

'The olden days,' she said.

'That's right,' he said, grinning though probably not so as she'd notice. 'The olden days.'

What they'd noticed the previous night and were again in full evidence were the stars – in places almost filling every inch of sky. She asked about the brightest one he thought was called Sirius. And then another that was hovering midway between two far-off galaxies.

All very different from home. Just as the heat was different from home. Along with the sea and the hot dry sand. And bathing in outdoor pools.

But what both were quietly coming to accept – without it ever featuring as a major topic of conversation – was that it was shaping up to be *home* a good deal longer than they'd envisaged. A home devoid of push-button consumer luxuries their respective generations had come to take for granted. And – following events on-board ship – of greater complications that might easily have come their way.

Like the previous night the island had quickly descended into an eerie stillness. He wondered if a storm was on the way. It made him fidgety, the sound of their voices seeming exaggerated – possibly the only human voices for hundreds of miles. Another thought best not to dwell on as they took turns preparing for their second night in the cave. It wasn't a case of deliberately not talking about the prospect of being rescued. The incident on the ship would have registered somewhere, prompting a search in the immediate location and likely beyond, meaning that sooner or later help would undoubtedly arrive. But the best way to get through the day was not to ignore or refuse to mention it, but just to leave it at that – for now at least.

Only as he crawled into the privacy of his sleeping-bag for the second night running – did he allow the possibility to cross his mind that what he'd been imagining might not be the case at all.

The dawn of a new day brought renewed activity on the far side of the cave.

'I think it's hotter than yesterday.' Like the previous day she was already up and around, looking his way whilst leaning on the cave wall, a hand drawing imaginary traces of sweat from her brow.

'Tea?' He watched her turn, leaning with her back to him to lift the pan of water onto the gas ring.

'Careful,' he said.

Following breakfast he stated his intention of making a quick trip to the beach. Though unlikely to reveal anything of note it would see them through the first part of the morning – a means of keeping busy or being seen to keep busy.

She announced her intention of joining him. She still didn't like the idea of spending time on her own and the idea of an early morning dip in the sea sounded appealing.

Like the previous days, it was a cloying heat that accompanied them on their descent from the cave. A heat causing the leaves of trees to droop limply from branches in places only a few feet above them. She commented on them and he told her about the mugga-wood tree found in Australia: a symbol for a broken heart, its flowers set with a substance resembling blood. She grimaced and left him a moment to take hold of one of the leaves, weighing it gingerly in one hand. It was surprisingly heavy. She let it drop, attempting – though not entirely succeeding – to avoid leakages seeping onto her top and shorts. Staring up at a panorama of green.

'It's beautiful,' she remarked. 'Don't you think?' He joined her beneath what, on close viewing, would certainly rate as one of the island's most distinctive features.

In the space close to the sea they parted company. Still wary – he watched her race across the sand, hurrying to avoid wasting time in getting to the water. Beyond which – for the third day running – nothing stirred. The sky, the sea, the thin haze that blended the two – exactly as they'd left it the day they'd arrived.

Content to leave her to it – he turned to his spot in the shadow of trees bordering the beach. A position awarding him a decent view of sea and sky, and on taking his seat – a hand waved above the water-line some way from the water's edge. He waved back. The least he could do – and probably the only activity to be spotted that day along the entire length of coastline.

She resurfaced to find him laid back on the grass: the classic sunbather's pose of closing his eyes, head turned to the sky.

Aware of her approach, he turned a squinting eye in her direction. She was towelling herself down and shaking excess water from a mane of hair, even huger when wet. Only when dry did she slide the shirt over her shoulders and pull the shorts back into place.

'All right?' she asked.

'Fine,' he said, slowly getting to his feet and looking to where the dinghy was still visible perched a few yards from dry land.

With the bulk of the island investigated there was little to discover that would likely be to their advantage. The only bit they'd barely touched was a bit that from a distance didn't seem too accessible – a rocky promontory jutting into the sea on the far eastern corner. They agreed they might as well take a wander in that direction. They may come across some other fruit trees or maybe ponds with fish and crabs though the business of catching them would be an issue, particularly fish. Not to mention cooking them. The only cooking facility being the single ring Calor-Gas camping-stove and a small saucepan.

The promontory was more rocky than on their side of the island, each step requiring help to avoid slipping, sliding or stumbling over rocks in some places up to half their height. But it was definitely the terrain for rock-pools which – once within touching distance of the sea – proved to be the case in just about any direction you cared to look.

They stopped to check which might prove most productive. What they both noticed was the difference in the sea – in this part of the island more choppy and restless than on their side; along with the rocks – making the prospect of swimming a non-starter. Not that it stopped her suggesting it. But on this occasion he was adamant. No way was she going to go diving into the sea in these parts.

'I'll be careful,' she said.

'You won't need to be,' he said.

It was the first time she'd detected a teacher's tone of voice.

'Is it because you're frightened I'll get hurt?' she asked.

He looked to where sprays of silver dashed against rocks before finally settling in eddies and whirlpools out of sight from where they were standing.

'Something like that,' he said, steadying himself from slipping whilst aiding her balance with a free hand.

'Suppose I refused and went ahead?' she said.

'I don't think you'd do that,' he replied.

She hung onto his hand, not in too much of a mood – or mind – to press him on it.

'Whatever you say sir,' she said.

'Good,' he said. 'So – let's forget swimming and check out a few of these pools.'

They helped each other across a string of seaweed-strewn boulders, in places feeling their way and taking a break every now and then to examine which might be of sufficient width and depth to be home to reasonable sized fish.

They came to the first of two pools, the steeper rocks mostly behind them. They looked down, searching for signs of life – at first seeing only masses of seaweed clinging to two to three feet beneath the surface. Then – seconds later – three fish clearly visible darting in and out of plankton.

'We need a pointed stick,' he said, releasing her with an instruction to head along what was a relatively safe route to the nearest trees to find a stick with a point on it.

'How sharp a point?' she asked.

'Sharp enough,' he said. 'But not so sharp as to stab yourself with it.'

She turned to head in the direction he was indicating.

'Because you're frightened I'll hurt myself,' she said.

'That's right,' he said.

'What about the fish?' she said. 'You don't care about hurting the fish.'

'No – I *do* care about hurting the fish. That's why I want you to go and find a pointed stick.'

He watched her stride off.

'Be careful,' he shouted after her, though already a few rocks away she'd probably fail to catch what he was saying.

'Yes sir,' she said, deliberately elongating the *sir*. Whilst aware she was more than likely speaking entirely to herself.

Determined not to return empty-handed, it took some searching to find the stick she guessed was up to the job.

'I got this,' she said, returning minutes later waving a three foot stick but not sure which end constituted the pointed end.

'Is it sharp?' he asked. She examined both ends.

'Kind of…' she said. Fortunately they had an all-duty penknife at hand discovered in one of the crates usually carried with them in case of emergencies. 'Right,' he said, handing her the finished article. 'All you've got to do now is stab one of the fish.'

They were stood on a rock bordering the pool, waiting for whichever fish was about to make itself visible. They didn't have to wait long; two appeared, both hovered motionless for a moment. She contemplated which would be her best bet, aware she didn't have much time to come to a decision.

'How do I do it?' She had the stick clutched in the style of a javelin thrower.

'Just aim at it – or ahead of it if it seems like it's about to move.'

'How do I know which way it's going to go?'

'Assume forwards,' he said.

'What about if it doesn't move?'

'Then aim straight at it,' he said.

'Do I stab it or throw it?'

'Whatever comes natural, or seems easiest,' he said. 'And keep your voice down. You don't want to frighten it.'

'I think stabbing it would be best,' she said. He agreed.

Whatever the grounds for optimism both knew the chances of success were minimal. And that it barely mattered. What mattered was they were passing time; another five minutes, another hour...another day.

Time spent, working together as teacher and pupil – engaged on an activity that mattered only in being seen to make a fist pursuing it.

With all the time in the world – and a hand to guide her – she made three or four stabs in the direction of one of the fish.

'Shit!' What luck she'd had had finally abandoned her – the fish vanishing from the scene the second she'd made contact with the water; the expletive intended mainly for her ears though not entirely. He watched from over her shoulder.

'You need to be quicker,' he said. She decided it was his turn.

'Your turn,' she said. He was the teacher. Maybe he would show her how it should be done. He took the stick, the point hovering close to the surface of the water. But the fish, along with most other creatures in the vicinity – were no fools. Whoever these strange visitors to their island were – they were neither huntsmen nor fishermen.

'You're useless,' she said, but without any inclination to seize the stick for a second attempt.

Reaching a point following a three foot climb they sat a while watching the ocean. The water was a dark blue colour, in places almost black. The waves turbulent, headed by trails of white foam that mysteriously disappeared before crashing onto the first line of rocks.

'It's beautiful,' she said. 'If I had my smartphone I could have taken a photo.' As far as he could recall, it was the first mention of mobile phones since their first day. An observation he might have shared but had little to add to. Fortunately – no more than did she.

Though clearly a prime spot to have parked themselves – it seemed wise not to hang around too long. It was difficult to gauge the tide that might be on the move and the last thing they needed was to find themselves stranded.

They headed back taking a different route, following a corner of the island more rugged than their stretch of coast, eventually coming to a stop by a shallow pool, alongside which a large crab was scratching around probably in search of food and, unlike the fish, definitely there for the taking.

They stopped to watch. Catching it would be child's play. How you went about killing it could wait. Maybe a swift bash against a rock.

Kim was on her haunches, lifting it by its shell, loving the sight of its legs or claws waving manically in search of something solid to latch onto. There'd be the question of cooking it, shelling it first and trying to decide which bits you ate and which bits you chucked away – bits currently flailing in just about every direction. From where they were stood – a more convoluted business than was warranted – even cruel. A conclusion meeting agreement a few feet away. Still kneeling, she released it, watching it scramble to what it rightly regarded as its natural habitat. The crab – along with the fish – would live to see another day.

'Lunch' continued to consist of one of the vacuum-packed bars along with fruit picked from the trees – a supply in need of replenishment before the day was over. It was following a suggestion they return to the trees that Kim announced her intention of taking an afternoon dip. In the next breath – suggesting he join her. Ostensibly an innocent enough suggestion though in light of recent developments, a decision not to be taken lightly.

Viewed from a distance, her recent predilection for swimming topless was neither here nor there. But with only a few feet between them it wouldn't be quite that simple. It wasn't that he was prudish or had any hang-ups about such things. And they *were* several thousand miles from home. None of which detracted from the fact that he was her teacher and she was his pupil.

Considerations getting short shrift from Kim. Her arm hooked through his, she escorted him to a point just short of the waterline. Where – without a hint of embarrassment or hesitation, first the shorts – and then the top were removed and dropped onto the sand.

Obliged to follow, he watched her lower herself into the water – drawing his top off his shoulders. The shorts would stay exactly where they were.

Shoulder deep, she turned, beckoning him to follow. He waded slowly – opting for a more cautious approach. But it felt good. And sinking slowly into the water he swam to within a few feet of where she was treading water on her back, her eye fixed on the sky.

He mirrored her movements, allowing his hands to be seized for a quick shoulder-deep ducking before moving off in search of deeper waters where they parted company, leaving him to pass time treading water while she swam to some twenty to thirty yards away.

Back on dry land some way ahead of her, he watched her emerge from the water – sticking to his policy of averting his gaze as she dried herself down only feet away. Only when it was time to clamber back into shorts with the top firmly in place did she reach for his hand, pulling him to his feet – encouraging him not to feel his age in his attempt to keep up with her on the hike back to the cave. Though for once he suggested she go on ahead. He wanted to do a quick check in the dinghy and would catch up with her later.

Alone for the first time in a while, he made the quick detour to where the dinghy was, not surprisingly, exactly as they'd left it, checking above and beneath the seats for any reserve gas-canisters that might have been overlooked first time round.

On confirming little remained to be discovered, he headed back via a different route taking him within touching distance of the waterfall, in places slowing him to a snail's pace, the steeper ascents awarding a clear view of darker clouds moving in from the east, making him wonder if they might be in for a little rain, something they'd yet to experience.

Back at the cave – he checked inside and down the slope towards the pool. There was no sign of Kim. He checked again, taking one of the water bottles under the pretence of filling it whilst expecting to find her crouched by the pool having beaten him to it.

By the waterfall he leant to fill the two bottles. There was still no sign of her. On the way back he took a slight detour to see if she was up on the ridge, possibly taking in the view down the steeper approach to the sea. There was no sign of her there which could only mean she was busy with some activity that took her further afield. Possibly a sketch she'd been meaning to do of one or more of the trees' leaves.

He made his way back, negotiating the bracken that allowed a shortcut back to the cave. There was no sign of life in or around the entrance or inside. Maybe she'd spotted or heard something in the trees and had set off to investigate. Or maybe just a toilet visit: an arrangement they'd worked out by cordoning-off an area of trees with ribbon and using a small trowel found at the rear of the dinghy.

Whatever it was, she was taking her time. Fifteen minutes became twenty-five minutes which rapidly became forty minutes.

He sat in the entrance, for the first time aware of a sense of solitude. They'd had moments to themselves over the last few days but this was the first time either of them had gone anywhere for any length of time and without explanation or apparent reason. He didn't begrudge her a little time to herself. It wasn't as if she was obliged to seek his permission for her every move. But it didn't quite fit with her usual way of doing things.

Occupying himself proved difficult. He checked the gas canisters, took his sketch pad and added a few notes, limiting himself to observations about the weather and the prospect of rain. But restlessness quickly kicked in and on the stroke of the hour – anxiety began to take over.

Something was going on and hanging around waiting for her was achieving nothing. He needed to *do* something; to start searching. She could have tripped, sprained an ankle or – though he baulked at thinking about it – something far worse.

Reaching the ridge he stopped to look in each direction, getting close to the plum trees before stopping to consider his next move – resisting the temptation to shout her name. It probably wouldn't do any good and would smack of a sense of anxiety he was eager to keep at bay.

That he was heading in one of any number of directions she might have taken was clearly an issue. Maybe, on reflection, his best move would be to be to stay close to the cave. Knowing that wherever she'd been and whatever she'd been up to – he'd be around when she returned.

It was twenty or thirty yards short of the entrance that he detected some movement and seconds later, spotted her sitting, knees drawn, peering in the direction of the sea. Aware of movement behind her she swung round.

And in an instant, realised she'd overstepped the mark. An admonishment that wouldn't have been out of place at school, would perhaps suffice. Confirmation that – by his own admission – current circumstances bore no relation to school. That for now, at least – things were different

Instantly on her feet she stumbled for an explanation.

Struggling – for once under pressure to find the words. That she just wanted a little time on her own though not wanting to couch it in quite those words. Eager to avoid the implication she'd needed time away from *him*. Beyond which – with a fully crestfallen expression – she admitted to having lost all track of time.

He was staring in the direction of a strip of beach between sea and sky. What he felt wasn't so much anger as a feeling that something going back as far as their arrival on the island had been put to the test.

'I was worried,' he said. 'I thought something might have happened___'

'I know,' she said. 'I'm sorry.'

She followed him to the rear of the cave where he took two plastic cups and a tea-bag.

'Your turn to make the tea,' he said.

He watched her turn, and without comment take the pan of water to the cooking-ring. 'I just lost track of time,' she said.

'It's okay,' he said, wanting and realising he needed to believe her.

It was at the onset of afternoon that he did a quick calculation on the remaining tins of food. On current rations of a tin a day they'd be okay for a week, maybe a week and a half. But the ship's Emergency Supplies were designed to be no more than that: an aid to survival in the event of needing to abandon ship until such time as help – in whatever guise – appeared on the scene. A quicker calculation meant they'd be looking at ten to fourteen days assuming they made each tin last two days, before alternative sources of sustenance would need to be considered and assuming an open tin would last twenty-four hours. The gas cylinders were less of an issue and they still had a healthy supply of the cereal bars and fruit they could count on for the foreseeable future.

All – he was still telling himself – likely to prove academic. Whatever the shortcomings of the authorities, he knew rescue services would spring instantly into action when it came to missing school-parties, even over a radius stretching several hundred miles. These things were bound to take time. It was just a question of waiting.

He'd also thought about the ship's dinghies. With at least one missing, it was surely logical to think in terms of there being survivors.

All thoughts kept to himself for now. He'd give it two to three days before putting the idea of rationing to her, just to be on the safe side.

In the more immediate future, afternoon awaited. Despite the threat of rain – an afternoon hike had been suggested.

Originally her idea, though in light of events – a suggestion he'd agreed to go along with.

Armed with a bottle of water and half a biscuit each, they took their usual route heading past the ridge in the direction of the rock-pools though probably not intending to get that far. Instead taking an alternative path where the leaves that continued to attract her attention tended to be more plentiful.

Like before, she found time to weigh them in her hand, warming to their size and almost leathery texture. Seeing her re-engaged with the surroundings was reassuring. A return to normality that a few hours ago might have been under threat.

A sparser area followed, the trees thinner in density through which an increasingly leaden sky was clearly visible. Were rain to arrive the leaves probably offered as good a means of protection as any, though it would unlikely be much of an issue. It wasn't the same as at home where getting soaked could interrupt your whole day's agenda. Since arrival on the island, whatever clothing had been worn had been minimal and were they to get wet they'd simply get back and change. The emergency clothing allowed a two day cycle though they'd got in the habit of washing the previous day's clothes first thing in the morning to dry during the course of the day.

He actually warmed to the prospect of a bit of rain. He'd be interested to see what form it took in these more remote latitudes. The only downside: something he'd failed to consider – how the dinghy would bear up, particularly in the event of an absolute downpour. Its seaworthiness had never been in question and though the likelihood of it being put to the test again was slim, there was something reassuring about having it sitting there just in case: a potential means of escape, if only in theory. Whilst not dismissing the possibility of needing it to get them *to* a rescue ship as opposed to the ship getting close enough to land to rescue them.

It took about ten minutes to return to where it remained exactly as they'd left it. He thought he'd seen a cover which, on delving under the counter at the top end he withdrew from its packaging: a polythene sheet designed to cover the whole seating area. With her help it was soon in place, secured at regular points by tying nylon round the loops on the perimeter.

By the time they'd returned to their spot beyond the ridge the skies were about ready to burst – casting a silvery, almost ghostly pall over the entire length of land. Clear hint that what was to follow might be something out of the ordinary and that they'd do well to be prepared for.

The first drops arrived as they stood at the head of a slope on what passed as a path though there was no way it could be strictly regarded as such.

Seconds later, occasional drops became a drumbeat of pellets pattering the nearby leaves.

She stepped back – her head held back to feel the splashes raining down on her forehead, her eyes by this stage firmly closed.

What followed was beyond anything experienced at home – the whole island seemingly at the point of being entirely submerged.

Still out in the open, semi-blinded by the rain but with no option other than to care not a jot – she grabbed his hand, hauling him down the slope towards the trees, her hair reduced to sodden streaks clinging to close-to bare shoulders.

And with every step she was calling, it became more difficult to hear...

Until – clinging to an arm in an attempt to shield the inevitable contact with a tree – they stumbled the last few yards, coming to a halt in a virtual clinch; a sodden top and equally sodden skirt offering minimum insulation; her waist – he realised all too quickly, but inevitably – firmly in his grip. As – a few inches higher and seconds later – were the twin pyramids of her breasts pushing through the soaking top into his rib-cage.

He turned – an involuntary thrust of an arm seeking to put distance between them.

Clambering his way to the tip of the slope. Where, seconds later from somewhere below, half lost in the rain – a voice sounded___

'Sir...You don't have to go...' Arms clung to a tree, shouts raised to compete with the now driving rain.

But it came too late. Even before speaking she realised she was talking only to the leaves and pools of rainwater rapidly gathering round her feet.

Slowly – she made her way to the top of the slope – from which point there was only one direction to be heading. A route – by now almost as familiar as the path to her front door at home – and, on this occasion, with little need to hurry.

It was twenty or thirty yards short of the entrance that she spotted the rear of his head to the left of the entrance, the hair – untypical for the times – worn close to touching his collar-bone. He was staring at the ground between land and sea.

Without waiting for an invitation, she took her place beside him.

He felt an arm creep to just below his neck where it came to a halt.

'It's all right,' she said. 'It's not your fault. None of what's happened is your fault.'

She was staring at the nape of his neck – on this occasion neither seeking nor expecting a reaction.

'And I'm not just talking about what happened down by the trees.'

She followed his gaze to where the thin line of sea met a host of angry-looking clouds. She looked back.

'I'm talking about *everything* that's happened.'

The roles – for once – seemed to have reversed. She was peering through strands of sodden hair, not wanting the moment to go unnoticed.

'Think about it – the way things have happened. Finding this place, then the cave, the waterfall, the trees...ponds, crabs, fish___'

Smoothing hair from her face, she took his hand, following his eye in the direction of the sea. She leant – half looking into his face as if anticipating a reaction.

'Don't worry…everything's going to be fine,' she said.

Seconds later she was on her feet, pausing temporarily at the cave's entrance before disappearing from sight.

With a final glance at the deserted miles of sea, he got to his feet – resigned to joining her.

* * * * *

Post Script

The optimistically (and maybe 'euphemistically') named 'Queen Of The Seas' ship [formerly a merchant vessel converted to accommodate fee-paying passengers on acquiring new ownership] went missing under mysterious circumstances on a May afternoon in 2007. Details of the incident continue, to this day, to be a mystery though evidence suggests an explosion of some sort, possibly in the engine room, occurred shortly after midday. The explosion caused extensive damage and the loss of over fifty lives, including pupils and teachers of a comprehensive school in Essex, England. The cause of the explosion remains a mystery, the possibility of terrorist activity not entirely discounted but unsubstantiated and deemed – under the circumstances – to be extremely unlikely.

On arrival at the ship's last known position, the search for the ship and any potential survivors was quickly underway – but after several days reported nil success. Whilst traces of the ship had been recovered, there were deemed to be no survivors.

Examination of what documentation survived revealed numerous flaws in safety procedures – one being a failure to keep an inventory of emergency equipment, including dinghies equipped with emergency supplies – a 'condition' of the ship's new ownership. Whether the dinghies would have been of any

*practical aid to those on-board is difficult to ascertain –
records proving to be non-existent. Further examination of
the scene confirmed that survival of some passengers might
have been possible.*

*Five weeks after the incident the search for any survivors
officially drew to a halt.*

When In Berlin

Berlin's streets were cold and getting colder by the minute – people's breathing visible a good few feet ahead of them, cast against a backdrop of lights and pre-Christmas shop windows.

The man clad in a long double-breasted coat hunched into his collar on emerging from his hotel, pulling his scarf and his hat tight whilst repeatedly checking the pocket of his bag.

He checked again with his watch. *Aschingers* could wait a while. *Bahnhoff-Zoo* could wait till tomorrow except for buying his ticket. He'd get that sorted now. He knew sufficient German to deal with it, hopefully without causing too much consternation on the far side of the counter – the response likely to be a few words he'd either understand or not need to understand. Unlike arriving at the hotel – a back street joint close to the *Ku'damm* where, unlike the fancier hotels, they didn't bother about you filling out forms. And on trying his bit of German with the guy behind the counter, as usual having it backfire on him when he insisted on saying something back to him. Which, as usual, he didn't understand, prompting an instant switch to English – on both sides of the counter!.

Crossing a maze of streets and traffic-lights, he found the kiosk opposite *Bahnhoff Zoo* station. Back on the street a few minutes later with his seven-day travel ticket tucked firmly in his top pocket. He'd negotiated that no problem. No-one had even attempted to speak back to him.

Next on the agenda – the Kneipe on the corner opposite, where – unless things had changed – they served *Kostritzer.*

The only way to get a trip to Berlin off the ground: at least two *Kostritzers* in the bar opposite *Bahnhoff Zoo*.

It was exactly as he'd pictured it: the string of beer-mats above a line of smokers huddled in conversation, the *Herta-Berlin* football pendant, the filling of glasses timed to perfection. Sue had liked this bar. Though not as much as the one at *Nikoleiviertal* or the one just off *Wittenberg Platz*. Maybe because it was the first place they'd set foot in.

Occupying a stool beneath the window, the memories came flooding back. Mostly good. Sufficient to have him raise his glass. To Berlin. And to everything that might transpire on his current visit to it.

He did a quick check on the staff. Both males in their late twenties or early thirties. He couldn't remember if they were there before. He wondered if they were brothers. Not that it mattered. Apart from which, this wasn't on his list. And it was too early.

He drank and was soon at the point of ordering another beer. Next was the issue of where to eat. *Aschingers* was a possibility. Sue had liked eating there. Goulash or Erbsen Suppe if he remembered rightly. If in doubt faced with a German menu, go for the goulash or the *Erbsen-Suppe*. The beer was good too, as it tended to be in these *Haus-brauerei* places.

He drank up. He'd hit one more bar – find a place he'd never been to before, and maybe head for *Aschingers* later.

He found a place hidden behind one of the side-streets, one of those shabby-looking places that usually turn out to be okay once you're inside. He ordered and took a seat watching a fair-haired young woman in jeans joking with a man on a bar-stool old enough to be her grandad, both giving the impression he was teasing her about something or maybe flirting with her but only in the way older men got to flirt with younger females working behind bars. And her probably knowing him well enough not to take any offence in what he was saying. That it was just a bit of harmless banter.

He lit a cigarette and was tempted to time how long it'd take to fill the glass. *Zieben Minuten Pils...*Seven minute Pils. Supposedly how long it takes to repeatedly top-up the glass. More memories that – for the time being – were set to remain little more than that. And – for the time being – he was happy to hang onto...along with other stuff: the bars, the U Bahn rides. *Savigny Platz, Wittenburg Platz.*

Only later would things be different.

Back on the street he paced his way to the U Bahn station. Five stops and there'd be no problem getting the right line with only two platforms to choose from. He pulled his hat tight and checked his wallet. And his travel ticket tucked in his top left pocket.

The smells hit you the minute you reach the steps. Rubber mixed with soot. Every subway in every city on the planet has that smell. He liked the smell. It reminded him of being a foreign city; alone but still part of the scene. On the move but with a sense of purpose.

He was heading east. And had to wait approximately fifty seconds for the first train to appear. He'd timed its arrival on his watch. Something he often did when travelling the U Bahn in this city.

It wasn't a long journey. He'd worked the route out beforehand: changing at *Hallesches Tor.* He was fairly sure he could remember the pub. He had a good memory for pubs though not always for their names.

Climbing the steps from the station he pulled his hat tight and his coat tighter. It was colder away from the centre. He breathed into a hunched up collar but it didn't make much difference. A biting wind struck his forehead. Recollections of his last visit told him it was a left and then a right turn. Which a few yards along a street a good deal shabbier than closer to the centre, seemed to ring a bell. A big building on the corner – confirmation he was on the right track.

He turned into the street trying to remember the first time they'd been there. It hadn't been the last visit. Maybe the May tour. Getting off the U Bahn one afternoon to stretch their legs, coming across the place and deciding to rest their feet for a while.

He spotted the pub. The sign visible the minute you crossed the street. *Zum Tante Una* or whatever the last word was. He often had a problem with the last word of German pub names... *Venue one* on his list.

He pushed the door, insulated along the bottom to keep out the cold. Cigarette smoke and raised voices accompanied him to the bar. He eyed the beer options, a *Ko-Pi* seeming the best bet. He placed his order and took his seat. There were three staff – one female. The two males appeared to be Turkish, probably early thirties. A few minutes later he took the drink from the bar and turned to his seat. One guy looked round, neither had made an attempt to communicate with him which wasn't too surprising. He watched the procedure for filling a line of glasses: the froth wiped clear with a spatula. The taller of the two guys seemed to be the busier. Both had moustaches and engaged in small-talk with each other, possibly brothers, not that it made any difference.

With the glass half empty and on giving it five minutes, he left his seat and approached the bar. He took the photo from the bag and urged the man to step closer to view it from close range.

He watched him dealing with something beneath the counter whilst eyeing the picture. Watched it take a moment for him to break into a smile and extend a hand, calling across for his friend or brother whoever it was to step over for a minute. A moment of recognition he found reassuring. Though that was as far as it went.

He joined in a bit of banter, but only briefly. They hadn't asked about Sue which – in this bar – didn't matter too much and wasn't any great surprise. In these places people rarely took liberties by asking questions. But they'd remembered her, which was nice. He retook his seat and put the picture back in its zip pocket. He checked the other bit of the bag and his watch. There'd be time for one more before heading for the next bar – the last before getting back to *Savigny Platz.*

It meant two changes taking him to a bar on one of the streets close to *Friedrichstrasse* – a place they'd found one afternoon spent traipsing in and out of museums and an art gallery not far from *Anhalter Bahnhoff.* Not exactly his idea of fun but tolerable if followed by a couple of beers.

Like before, he found the street no problem – and more or less recognised the pub from the sign. Not that he could read it; it was too high and too dim.

The place was noisy. And smelt of cooking. One of the bar staff he definitely recognised, the other appeared to be new. No-one noticed his approach to the bar where, on his arrival, the man he remembered immediately extended a hand. All indications were that this too would be fairly straightforward. Chance to tick *venue-two* off his list.

He took the photo from the bag and held it for viewing from behind the bar, the barman smiled, asking something he didn't quite catch. He invited the others to come and take a look. Soon three and then four people were on the scene. Another comment followed. He couldn't catch what was said but it probably wasn't for his ears. He was asked about Sue which got a shrug. He'd decided beforehand a shrug of the shoulders would be his stock response if questioned, on these occasions his lack of German more an asset than a liability.

He slipped the picture back in its zip-pocket and took his seat. There'd be time for one more before heading for *Savigny Platz.* Plus, he'd need to take his next tablet soon. He'd got them tucked in one of the pockets at the rear of his bag.

The bar at *Savigny-Platz* – he could never remember the name – was purely relaxation. They'd got to know the guy who owned it on a previous visit, a younger, busy guy by the name of Karl who – like a lot of guys working behind bars – never seemed to stand still; always in the midst of doing something or tending to someone. Constantly on the lookout for people needing to be served which was good when it got busy and succeeded in conveying the impression he was serious about what he was doing, keen to make the place a going-concern.

At his arrival a hand was raised and pointed questioningly at the *Guinness* tap.

It felt good to be acknowledged. Like being regarded as one of the regulars. And this pub was different from the others. 'Trendy' was a word some might use but it wasn't really the right word. Germany, or Germany cities – Berlin in particular – had loads of these bars: often darkly-lit, late-night places, music orientated, boldly painted walls lined with posters for *Dylan* or *Zappa*. Food available but only the quick-and-easy-to-serve stuff. The staff usually young and fluent English speakers.

The *Guinness* arrived. Not very Germanic but at this stage of the evening a welcome change from the *Pils*.

There'd be no need to get the photo out though he'd have liked to, if only for old time sake and for reasons having nothing to do with this visit. But it would stay in his bag. Sue had liked this place. Maybe being able to communicate helped. But also the music. And the fact it was open late. And that it served a drink she'd acquired a taste for. He couldn't remember what it was.

If asked about Sue he'd need to make it clear he had nothing to say. Which should get the message across. Karl, the guy who ran the bar was okay. He'd gather it was a subject not up for discussion. They'd got chatting to him on a number of occasions: about bands they'd liked, beer, other places in Germany, a few museums he recommended. Even bits of politics and his two or three visits to London.

The *Guinness* was good. Even by UK standards. And would do him for the night. He settled into his corner and reached for his bag.

Outside – the first snowflakes were beginning to fall.

Lightened by alcohol, he huddled into his coat and pulled his trilby-hat tight as he left the pub, his movements at first uncertain as he tried establishing a kind of rhythm, a careful placing of his feet to avoid sliding on an increasingly slippery pavement following a minor fall of snow – not always easy when you're pissed. But the street's lights would guide him in the right direction and serve as a welcome distraction, confirmation it hadn't been a bad night. And Karl had done the wise thing by not mentioning Sue which he was relieved about.

Back on the *Ku'damm* traffic appeared from nowhere behind trails of yellow light. The snow had failed to make any real impression, the streets sprinkled white only in parts next to the buildings furthest from the road. He tried to recall whether it had snowed when Sue had last been here. She always had a thing about freshly fallen snow. He could remember her going out with her camera once before breakfast and being out till near lunchtime. He seemed to recall meeting her in the hotel bar.

He found the hotel. He pulled his coat and leant into the revolving door. A quick 'hi' to the man on reception. A Turkish fellow by the look of him. Maybe he got to do most of the night shifts.

He'd slept okay. Ahead of him the daytime hours needed to be filled. Chance to get some mileage out of his Seven-Day travel-ticket. *Bahnhoff Zoo* was his first destination. Back to the smell of soot but in this case with a sweet edge like candy-floss. Plus, sausages frying. No major German Bahnhoff's atmosphere was complete without the waft of sausages frying somewhere in its vicinity.

He checked the line having a pretty good idea what connections would be needed. Trains rattling in and out by the second was a reminder you were at the hub of the city's transport system. He liked the older carriages, the rickety wooden jobs with benches for seats – a bit of old-Berlin though probably as much to do with financial prudence as any act of posterity. A mother struggled with a pram and three children into the carriage. He'd have liked to offer to help, knowing exactly what to say, but she was foreign – probably east European or Turkish and he wasn't sure how the offer would be received. And she was on-board before he'd got round to it.

The first U Bahn on the first morning was a moment to savour. A curve in the line giving a decent view as you exit the station: the graffiti'd gable-ends of tenement blocks replaced by what remained of The Wall poking from building-sites like half decorated shards of teeth. He'd have liked to see it in the old days with guards eyeing you through binoculars. He'd seen the photos and the pictures in the museum – guys hiding in boots of cars or gliding across the border down ropes slung from tenement blocks.

Alexander Platz and *Nikolaiviertal* were first on the list. Sue had liked *Nikolaiviertal*; particularly the waiters dressed in long maroon smocks; no doubt another attempt to recreate a bit of old Berlin. He took a seat at the café on the corner with the river close at hand. One of Sue's favourites. Probably because of the river. He couldn't remember the name of the river. But then he never bothered with the names of rivers. In fact, he never bothered with rivers. Or bridges. Just occasionally – in London, pubs *next to* rivers or bridges where you could sometimes get a decent pint.

It was too cold to sit outside and there wasn't much free space inside. It reminded him of cafes in the smarter German cities, particularly Cologne. Places frequented by smart-looking women. Or women wanting to be considered smart-looking. And drinking beer. You didn't often get that in England. And smoking too. There was talk about bringing smoking in public places to an end in England which would likely give everyone in the business something to think about – and likely complain about.

Time for his first tablet of the day. To be taken with a drink of water. Four a day according to instructions. And according to the doctor. Fortunately this batch were the easy to swallow size.

Next on the agenda was the bit of Berlin that rarely featured on postcards. Reason enough to consider it a part worth visiting. He'd checked the lines earlier. At *Alexander Platz* you needed to check you'd got the right line. In this case, the S Bahn if he remembered rightly.

With temperatures already sinking to somewhere below freezing, it wasn't the time to be hanging around too long on station platforms. He'd timed it on his watch: a four minute wait – long enough in anyone's book before the chance to put a few miles behind you finally arrived. Watching through a graffiti'd window as buildings either side of the track begin to thin out – gradually giving way to lines of abandoned stations and disused railway sidings.

Taking you into what some would argue is the *real* East Berlin: stretches of tower-blocks and largely abandoned shopping precincts where – for generations of its citizens, life goes on unseen and largely unnoticed by the remainder of the city's inhabitants. A part rarely seen by the casual visitor. And – being a casual visitor – you rarely get noticed.

You'd struggle to find a castle or a fancy garden in this part of Berlin. Like you'd struggle to find a *Trafalgar Square or Hyde Park* at the eastern end of London's *District Line*. Only stations – fewer and further between than closer to the centre – midst concrete esplanades urging you not to wander too far; maybe a few hundred yards before turning back on your tracks to board a near-empty train for the return trip.

Which, for some odd reason, always seems to take a little longer. But worth the wait to have the more familiar icons of the city once again in your sights: the 'broken tooth', the dome of *Bahnhoff Zoo,* the bars, shops and tree-lined avenues: all ready and waiting from when he'd left them only a few hours ago: the bit of Berlin featured on postcards: where kids tripped repeatedly on skateboards and guys wearing vaguely Eastern expressions stood by stalls laden with bits of The Wall stuck on plastic plinths – as much a monument to the modern-day consumer Berlin as anything found hanging on the walls of galleries.

But – with time still to kill – it would do. Except that, as often happens towards the end of the afternoon, you tend to run short on ideas. Too late to go far. Too early to go back to the hotel. *Wittenberg Platz* was a possibility: an historic station restored to its 'pre-war' classical look. He knew that because he'd read about it with it being Sue's favourite station. That, and the sign outside listing the concentration-camps – 'lest we ever forget'. A sign most people don't appear to notice any more.

A couple of hours later it's time to hit the streets once again. Shoulders hunched into his collar, he once again headed for the U Bahn.

He liked the older pubs – in this case the oldest pub in Berlin, which, if only for its off-the-beaten-track location was always worth a visit. But like any city's most celebrated venues, was inclined to get busy. Though the thing about places like this is that people barely notice you. He could watch them from his seat in the corner, but they barely knew they were being watched. Smart-looking women too like in the café earlier. Smarter – and often older than you'd get in English pubs. Sue had liked this pub. Another bit of 'Old Berlin'. Said it made her feel safe, secure. Needless to say, it was *not* one of the pubs on his list.

Ninety minutes after his arrival he'd seen off a plate of bratwurst and sauerkraut and five glasses of whatever beer he'd been drinking – he was getting too pissed to notice its name, and he could never remember the names of half the beers anyway. The place was filling up to a point of getting claustrophobic. He wasn't keen on busy pubs. People tended to be too close. Even pissed he preferred to keep his distance. Paying would again be no trouble. He'd had paying bills off to a fine art for some time now, the trick being to round it up by adding a bit on for a tip. And in these places people rarely spoke back at him.

Outside he pulled the collar tight and began to pace himself, like the previous night but with fewer lights and without the snow.

Getting to *Prenzlauer Berg* wasn't as straightforward as some places but no huge problem, or distance. In this city there were no huge distances to be covered or difficulties getting there. He knew both places were close to the main thoroughfare. Not too far to walk in near freezing temperatures.

At this time of night, an eight minute wait for the train came as no surprise. Chance to check the connections and remind himself of the lie of the land on arrival.

It was over half an hour later, descending steps to a street as bleak as the buildings lining it, that he recognised a Turkish fast-food place on the corner, then a right turn about fifty yards up the road.

He recognised the pub instantly. Stepping inside, this was definitely the place. Two males were behind the bar. Plus a female collecting glasses along a line of recently vacated tables. He lifted his hat and tried to shake some feeling back into his limbs. He looked again, checking whether either face behind the bar rang any bells. He recognised the guy on the left. Youngish – thirty to thirty-five or thereabouts. Lean-looking with one of those walrus moustaches you get a lot of in Germany. He was filling a glass, looking over his shoulder where the woman collecting glasses was back to placing fresh glasses beneath a line of taps.

He took a few steps closer. A seat on the left seemed a good bet to park himself for twenty minutes or so. Was it one of those places where you ordered at the bar? You could never be sure and he couldn't remember what happened last time. He'd checked the list of beers though he still couldn't recall the name of the pub. Not that it mattered. The names of places was irrelevant. All that mattered was it was *venue three* on his list.

He definitely recognised the man approaching and about to serve him. The same guy as last time; the flat, dead-pan expression you sometimes associated with eastern Europeans. If there was a flicker of recognition it didn't show. He waited till the glass was under the tap before calling him over, opening the zip-pocket of his bag in the process.

With their faces close to touching, he held the photo in one hand inviting the man behind the bar to take a good look. He looked, if only out of politeness, putting the glass to one side. Then mumbled something and called his colleague over. Both were struck by the girl's smile. And the hair – the flowing shoulder-length hair. Features people often made a point of commenting on in photos of her.

'Last winter,' one of them said, possibly taking the opportunity to practise his English, mouthing each syllable with an eye not to make any unfortunate slip-ups. He handed the photo to his friend for a closer look.

A few words passed before he pocketed the photo and waited for the beer to be delivered to the table as promised. By his calculations with this one ticked off the list there were another two to do.

Next was the place with the hanging curtains just inside the door. He wasn't sure of its exact location but reckoned he could find it by returning to the station and taking it from there.

Stepping outside was like stepping into an ice-box. He stood a moment, pulling the scarf into the collar of his coat, the hat pulled tight on his head.

Even in the depths of winter he liked this part of Berlin though he couldn't easily say why. Which was the same with many places. If asked why he liked them, he couldn't really explain it. It was difficult to come up with an obvious reason for liking any place; sometimes just a 'feel' he got about it. In this case – streets with a sense of identity borne out of being on the fringe of things; and being some distance [not necessarily in the geographical sense] from the better known parts of the city. For whatever reasons he'd quickly felt at home here as had Sue – though in her case partly on account of discovering a few galleries she'd read about in the guide and been told about. She had a thing about art galleries...and museums; spent half her life traipsing round the places...and graveyards. The Jewish cemetery had taken a bit of finding but – by all accounts had lived up to all expectations. He wouldn't know. To him such places were on a par with rivers and bridges. But there'd been occasions when he'd agreed to accompany her, knowing she preferred to view these things in company and wouldn't be too disheartened when her observations failed to get much of a response.

He straightened his hat and lifted the collar of his coat as he scoured the buildings opposite, looking for the tell-tale sign, then seeing a fork in the road ahead that told him it was a left turn. He remembered the lights. Like all traffic-lights in this part of the city – fat green men telling you to cross; fatter than on other lights.

He saw the sign about thirty metres ahead. The name rang a bell. He remembered the window as he got closer, the bullet-holes from the war, or what he assumed were bullet-holes still in evidence on the first floor above the entrance.

Venue four on his list. The door opened via the curtain he'd remembered into another low-lit interior that – not surprisingly on a night like this – was close to empty. Two males stood side by side behind the bar appearing to have anticipated his arrival.

The man on the left was definitely familiar. The one on the right he wasn't so sure about.

The man he was fairly sure he recognised watched his approach and turned to a line of glasses beneath the counter. He did his usual introductory bit in German.

Beers were pulled. In the process he reached into his bag and unzipped the pocket. On removing the photo from the bag, there was no reaction from behind the bar.

Only on closer examination did activity cease for a moment. He watched a head of foam being ceremoniously removed from the rim of the glass, the barman's eye focused exclusively on the task in hand.

'I remember,' he said, instantly turning away and holding the glass in place to catch the next pouring of beer. 'With Karl,' he added, making it sound almost an afterthought – an attempt to play down any possible implications.

He leant into the counter, urging the guy to stop what he was doing a moment – to repeat what he's just said, just to check he'd heard him correctly.

'Karl?' He repeated the name, looking down, busying himself beneath the counter. Confirmed with an exchange of nods, a towel folded casually over the second guy's arm.

He made his way to a nearby seat, knowing he'd need to go over every detail of their last trip. Particularly from five-thirty onwards, taking them to what had turned out to be their all-time favourite bar.

Which was when it all began to make sense!

Wandering off with her camera. Her parting shot – logical enough at the time – that she needed to be on her own. That she needed space and time to take pictures without distractions. Now he knew why. And why it had taken a sizeable chunk out of the last two afternoons...

He downed what remained of the *Pils* making a point of checking things two, three times. The photo was back in its place in his bag, his wallet, the hotel key in his top pocket. Turning to go, he had one more question.

How many times? Like going through the details of their last visit, it pained him to ask – but he needed to know. How many times had the woman in the picture and Karl been in the bar? He spoke in English. It wasn't the moment to be wasting time practising his German. Though even as he asked, another question was nagging away at him: an issue having little to do with the guys behind this the bar: Why pick a pub they'd visited together when there were a million other bars to choose from? Was he making a potential coincidence too much of an issue? The men again exchanged looks before replying.

Two, maybe three, was all they could – or *would* – say for sure. Stood side by side as if aware their disclosure was more than merely passing time, they watched him search his wallet to pay the bill before making his way back onto the street.

Where – for once – he barely noticed temperatures threatening to bring the entire city to a standstill.

With the early flakes of snow clearly visible though a halo of street lights – he set off in the direction of the station. His plan had been turned viciously on its head. But, no matter – what was done was done. An altogether redefined sense of determination drove him on. Turning the corner he pulled the collar tighter.

It was shaping up to be a long night. But in a way it was only just beginning...

For once the schlep from *Bahnhoff Zoo* was going to take time. But ne needed opportunity to think. He needed to have it all worked out in advance, and *time* – in all senses of the word – would be key.

Fortunately some things were in his favour. The weather for a start. A night when anyone stalking the streets would shrink into virtual anonymity.

It was on turning the corner, crossing the street and striding into a steadier onslaught of snow, that he came across an alley, which – on closer inspection – led to an apparently empty garage a good twenty yards off the street but with a clear view of the area just to the left of the pub.

Standing just inside the garage door that was partly open and could feasibly remain so, the lights of the main bar were visible though under no circumstances would he actually enter the premises despite the nagging temptation to do exactly that. But it would be a stupid move.

Almost as stupid as going from pub to pub – assuming guys working behind the bar would be sufficiently stupid – and sufficiently obliging to a virtual stranger – to give the game away by failing to acknowledge a photo. Even though, by a process of elimination, he'd figured it *had* to be someone working in one of the bars.

But this time – for once – he'd got it all planned. And on discovery of the garage – down to the finest detail.

He looked round. Thankfully there were no traces of snow, no danger of leaving footprints. His first move had been to walk back along the alley, stopping only to check in both directions before returning to the garage – effectively removing himself from public view.

Finding somewhere to park himself had been a huge plus. On closer viewing, a spacious enough spot to remain concealed amongst five or six large wooden casks. Who the garage belonged to was anybody's guess – if *anyone*. And at this particular moment, was of little consequence.

He stepped inside. Though still likely to be a test of his courage, not to mention survival technique – with the bar likely to close in half an hour or so, it wasn't as bad as being in the alley or out on the pavement with no protection from the elements whatsoever.

He checked the casks that were presumably there for a reason that, on a night such as this, was of little matter. All were empty. He checked the door. In the unlikely event of the garage owner turning up he'd simply get back on his feet, posing as someone seeking a little respite from the cold and happy to be on his way with no further questions asked.

He considered his best position – crouched behind one of the crates, knees drawn. The pavement opposite mostly in vision and almost able to see the bar door he knew his guy would be exiting before too long.

It had been an exhausting evening. And an emotional return to what – at one time – had been his favourite city – bar none.

But an end to his time there was now in sight. Not quite the end he'd envisaged – but a conclusion of sorts. The bit to follow – leading up to his departure by cab to the airport for the first flight home in the morning – had been scrupulously planned.

And now needed to be scrupulously prepared – particularly in the near Arctic conditions of the garage. But he'd be okay for half an hour or so, so long as he got his posture right. In these temperatures he needed to regularly readjust his position whilst keeping an eye on the door opposite. He'd have some warning: the lights of the bar going out – indication of his man about to leave the bar and turn to lock the door.

He reached for his shoulder-bag, clutching it tight to his chest – running his fingers along the handle sitting inside the bag's larger pocket.

He checked with his watch. He wouldn't have long to wait, hopefully no longer than thirty minutes, taking them to one-o-clock. Not for the first time he blew warm air into freezing fingers, taking some satisfaction in regarding this unpredicted and inhospitable hiding place as... *Venue Five* on his list.

Repeating it to himself as he drew knees to his chest, the bag clutched as if he could barely contemplate the idea of parting company with it; his final tablet of the day – for once destined to go unheeded.

Just as, back on the street – what had been a minor fall of snow was rapidly turning into a steady fall of full-size flakes.

In the bar almost opposite – it was turning out to be quite a night. Two birthday celebrations plus a party from Dusseldorf. The bar owner – barely having the opportunity to draw breath. It wasn't until something like 1:45 that, with food finally off the agenda, the pair had the opportunity to spend a little time with the customers. The topic of conversation – as in bars the length and breadth of the city – the icy temperatures that promised to sink to an all-time record low.

It was just after 3:30 am. that with the last of the punters ushered through the door, he turned his mind to a final task that ought to be done before they too departed the scene.

In the midst of washing the last batch of glasses, he turned to his partner, suggesting she take the keys from the hook and wrap up solidly even for the short trek across the road.

Pocketing the key and pulling her coat tight, she made her way onto the street – cheeks puffed to brace temperatures that few would likely survive for long outdoors. Planting her feet with care and seeking support along the side of the alleyway she approached the garage.

And with little reason or urge to hang around – assured the casks for loading stuff pending a move into the flat above the bar would be okay for a few days – she quickly pulled the metal door shut and padlocked it, pocketing the key before turning to retrace her steps.

Inside the garage a figure beyond vision, huddled behind the cask closest to the wall had barely moved for something close to ninety minutes; his face – a thin, ghostly hue; the look of a man whose plans might not quite have reached fruition – but had come pretty damned close.

'Okay?' The voice came from somewhere behind the bar.

'Yes fine.' She shook herself down, hanging key and then coat and hat on the nearest peg. 'There were a couple more boxes left near the door.'

He joined her in the now deserted bar, a glass of her favourite drink extended in one hand.

It had been a busy night but a lucrative one and with the mutual feel of a job well done, they clinked glasses and took the opportunity to take a seat in the corner.

It was close to four-thirty that the pair finally stepped onto a six inch snow-laden pavement, locking the door behind them before heading – head bowed – beneath the dim glow of street lights. She reached for his arm, her long flowing hair temporarily pulled into a bun beneath the Cossack-style hat.

At the lights they turned right heading for the station where – to the best of their knowledge – in something like five to six minutes the first U Bahn of the day should be arriving.

* * * *